TRUE BREEZE

A NAUTICAL NOVEL

BY
ED ROBINSON

This book is dedicated to a single-handed sailor named Shirley. She's in her eighties and still living aboard her tiny sailboat. Her stories about searching for gold have inspired this work.

Prelude

How hard does the FBI look for a fugitive? I needed to know because I'd just been informed they were coming for me. I'd been a wanted man before, but not by the FBI. I'd been on the run, but local law enforcement and the IRS weren't actively beating the bushes in search of me. They simply hoped that I'd turn up in connection with some other crime. Eventually, I did.

As for the embezzlement charge, I was able to beg for mercy and pay back what I'd stolen, plus interest. The IRS was happy to tack on many thousands in interest and penalties. I paid off my debt. The charge of possession of marijuana cost me a short stint in detention and a good deal of community service. I had fulfilled the terms of my probation. I was right with the law, until now.

My innocence was of no consequence. My ex-lawyer/ex-girlfriend had taken a bullet on a beach in the Bahamas. My current on-again, off-again love interest had pulled the trigger. She did it to save my ass. The only easy way out would be to reveal who really made the shot. I couldn't do that.

The gunshot victim had survived. She'd fingered me for the shooting. I'd gone out of my way to ruin her life. I'd exposed her as a criminal. I'd tracked her to the far ends of the earth. I thought I'd won. Instead, she'd turned the tables on me.

The bad news was that I'd have to run.

The good news was that I was damn good at it.

One

The freaking FBI! You've done it this time, Breeze.

I'd involved my friends in my personal revenge scheme. I'd taken pains to keep them out of harm's way. During the entire mission, I'd had a niggling feeling that something wasn't going to work out right. I'd even had a dream about it. We'd all survived unharmed, but something did indeed go wrong. Now the FBI was after me.

Taylor Ford had once been my lover. We'd met when she defended me against a charge of possession of marijuana. I was guilty as hell. She'd bribed a judge to keep me out of jail. I'd learn much later that she was a frequent dealer in the pay-to-play game that was south Florida politics. I'd unwittingly done her bidding in worse crimes. She used her sexuality to influence my decision making.

Holly was just the antidote. She was a carefree, rasta, hippie, sailor chick that I met down in the Cayman Islands. I hired her as crew to help me get back to Florida. She stayed on as my friend and confidant. We traveled the Bahamas together. Eventually, our relationship became a physical one. As hard as we both tried, it didn't work out in the long run.

Jimi D. had once been a trusted financial advisor. He got sucked in by Taylor too. He ran off with the millions that she had steered his way. Taylor wanted Jimi dead. I wanted her to face justice.

Holly, Jimi, and I set out to find her and bring her in. Everything went according to plan until the last second. Before Taylor could shoot me, Holly took her out with a quick shot from a nine- millimeter pistol. I'd forced Holly to run. I'd urged Jimi to take care of her. The two of them escaped while I stayed behind to save Taylor's life.

I should have let her die on that beach.

Taylor survived. Her first act upon waking up in the hospital was to accuse me of being her shooter. It wouldn't help her to escape justice, but it would certainly make my life more difficult. My selfish desire to beat her at her own game had backfired. She never saw the real shooter. She couldn't reveal the truth if she wanted to. I didn't want the truth to be known. I'd protect Holly's identity no matter what happened to me.

Holly was in the wind. She and Jimi D. had fled the scene aboard Holly's sailboat, *Another Adventure*. I'd made my way back to Florida and my old trawler, *Leap of Faith*. I spent a few days preparing the boat before I got the news. I still had Jimi's cell phone, hoping to hear from them. There had been no word yet. She was supposed to head for the Keys. I'd find her. I'd promised to find her.

Meanwhile, I needed to avoid being found myself.

As for the FBI, a quick Google search gave me some hope. If Taylor were cooperating with them, she'd tell them about my usual haunts. She'd tell them what my boat was named and what it looked like. They'd follow up, for a time. If they didn't find me or get a good trail, they'd give up the chase. My file would be forgotten until I was later arrested or otherwise turned up on the radar of some law enforcement jurisdiction. They'd send a man or two to poke around. Questions would be asked of known associates. Maybe a helicopter would fly over Pelican Bay and Fort Myers Beach.

Would they go to the Keys? It was possible, but the Keys are a good place to hide a boat. They'd probably check around Boot Key Harbor, which was Holly's likely landing spot. They weren't looking for Holly, though, they were looking for me. If I could avoid them for a month or two, they'd stop looking.

I needed to find Holly. I wanted desperately to find her. I needed to leave the marina where I'd been holed up. Taylor knew I was in the area. It wouldn't be hard to make a quick search of all the local marinas. There weren't that many to search. Jimi's boat was here too. He'd come back for it, but they weren't looking for him either. Holly and Jimi were free to do as they pleased, they just didn't know it yet.

I boarded Jimi's boat and wrote him a note. I used his phone as a paperweight to keep the note on his salon table. Once he arrived, he could call Holly to let her know not to worry about the cops chasing her down. He could tell her that I was on my way to the Keys. I'd find her. We'd disappear for a while. This shit would blow over. All I had to do was avoid contact with law enforcement for the rest of my life.

I felt familiar forces at work. My heart rate ticked up just a notch. I suddenly felt more aware of my surroundings. A tiny bit of adrenaline rush helped me get into motion. I was going on the run again, but I was running towards Holly. My preliminary mission was to avoid capture. My secondary mission was to reunite with the one person on earth that understood me. I'd have to figure out the rest of it later.

Leap of Faith was ready. I warmed up her single diesel engine and untied the lines. I'd forgotten how tight the slips were in that marina. I was going to need help getting out of there. I loosely re-tied two lines and walked the docks looking for a hand or two. The only folks milling about were Bobbie and Dave. They were a gay couple that I'd met previously at the pool. They lived aboard their sailboat,

Knot-T- Boyz. Their sexual orientation made no difference to me. They just seemed like nice people. Boaters, in general are a helpful bunch, so I asked if they could lend me a hand. They readily agreed.

With their help and some creative line tossing, I managed to get my boat out of the slip without hitting anything. They got me pointed in the right direction and I was free of the dock. After topping off with diesel at the fuel dock, I headed south on the ICW towards the Boca Grande Pass. I was grateful for the new drawbridge at Gasparilla Island. The old swing bridge had to open for *Leap of Faith* to pass through. I could go under the new bridge without it opening for me. I cruised behind the island and into the pass. The Gulf was calm, so I ventured offshore. Once clear of the markers, I turned south.

I debated with myself about stopping in Fort Myers Beach. It would be on the list of my known hangouts. I thought it would be wise to warn my friends there that the FBI might come snooping around. I wanted to ask them not to cooperate. On the other hand, I'd brought trouble their way more than once. Diver Dan had made it clear that he'd had enough of my adventures bleeding over into their peaceful existence. I decided against visiting them. They'd know what to do if someone came asking for me. It would be better if they hadn't seen me or known of my whereabouts.

I continued south past Estero Island and on to Marco. I checked the tides and decided that I could make it around the back way to Goodland. The sleepy little village would be a good spot to hide for the night. No one knew me there. No one would know to look for me there either. As I rounded the bend at the last marina in the basin, I saw a familiar boat. It was anchored just outside the break wall in shallow water. It was my old friend Shirley. I anchored nearby in deeper water. I had someone to talk to before moving on.

I'd first met Shirley in Pelican Bay. I was sitting on a beach when she ran her little boat right up onto shore. She plopped an anchor in the sand and jumped down holding a garden hoe. I watched as she proceeded to scrape barnacles with the hoe. She was wearing a one-piece bathing suit and a floppy hat. Her blonde-gray pigtails hung down on either side of her face. I learned that she was eighty years old. She was a tough old broad, except for when it came to sharks. She asked me to keep an eye out for them as she went into deeper water to scrape the back half of her boat.

I watched her work. She had arms like Popeye. Otherwise, she was a small thing. I learned that her arm strength was from daily rowing of her dinghy. I also learned that she couldn't afford to buy rum, but if I had some to share she'd certainly partake. We always sat, chatted, and sipped rum whenever we ran into each other. She sailed the west coast of Florida mostly, keeping to herself. She was a salty old cuss, and I respected that.

It was good to see her. I took my dinghy over to her boat to catch up.

"I see you finally got the nerve to come in the back door," she said. "Easy Peasy, like I told you."

"I had a good tide," I said. "How the heck are you Shirl?"

"Well, I gotta tell you," she said. "I ain't been doing so good."

She pulled her top aside, revealing a new scar.

"The doctor put a pacemaker in me," she said. "I think he's got it set on rocking chair mode. I ain't been right since I got this thing."

"Can they crank it up a notch?" I asked.

"I suppose they can," she said. "I went up the firehouse asking for help, but they said it wasn't no emergency. I've got to go back up to Englewood to see the doctor."

"You're going up there aren't you?" I asked. "Nothing to play around with."

"I'm going," she said. "Just not in a hurry. I hate doctors."

"I hear you," I said. "How've things been otherwise?"

"I'm glad you asked," she said. "You're just the person I need right now."

"Why? What's up?"

"I've been worrying about my mortality," she said. "There are some things I've been wanting to do, but I haven't been up to it physically."

"Something I can help you with?" I asked.

"Maybe," she said. "If I can trust you. I always thought I could trust you."

"I try to do right by my friends," I said. "The few that I have at least."

"I don't keep with too many friends either," she said. "People suck. I've got a daughter, though. She's never had too much time for her crazy old sailor mom, but I'd like to leave her something that would change her impression of me."

"I can't imagine what you're getting at," I said.

"Gold," she said.

"Gold?"

"Yes damn it," she said. "I know where there's some gold."

"You want me to go get it?" I asked.

"Hold on," she said. "I got something to show you."

Shirley went below. I heard her rummaging around. She came back up with a dish towel in her hands. She handed it to me. It was heavy. I unrolled the towel to find two rough gold blocks. They weren't bars or ingots. They were shaped more like a sardine can, and about the same size. There were no markings of any kind.

"There's more where those came from," she said. "But I can't get them."

"Why not?" I asked.

"Sharks," she said. "I had two more bars in my hand when a big bull shark came at me. I dropped them climbing in the boat. Sumbitch just about had me, Breeze."

"You think there's more than those two?" I asked.

"Who knows," she said. "I seen the glint of the sun on them bars. I was only in the water for a minute when the sharks showed up. I didn't go back down."

"The two you have should be worth a pretty penny," I said. "You want me to sell them for you?"

"I don't know," she said. "I keep dreaming of a pirate's treasure. I've been looking for Gasparilla's gold for twenty years. Maybe I found it."

"How'd you stumble onto this?" I asked.

"Fool tourists in a bar on Pine Island," she said. "They showed me a picture on one of them smart phones. They asked me what I thought it was. I said it looks like gold to me.

They said they thought so too. Wanted me to dive on it for them."

"Is that what you were doing?" I asked.

"Hell no," she said. "I told them no. They told me it was in the pass. Didn't say which pass."

"How did you find it then?

"That picture," she said. "It was open water in the background, but there was a marker in it."

"And you know those waters well enough to pinpoint the spot," I said.

"Damn straight I do," she said.

"Well?"

"Well, what?"

"Where is it?" I asked.

"You can't tell a soul," she said. "And if you run off with my gold I'll haunt your ass for eternity."

"You don't have to tell me," I said. "You can get it yourself. I can't steal it if I don't know where it is."

"You won't steal it will you, Breeze?" she asked.

"I don't really need the money," I told her. "But if there're millions laying down there, I wouldn't mind a cut."

"Keep half of whatever you find," she offered. "But I'd like you to sell those two first. I might not live long enough for you to make me rich."

"I've got to get to the Keys right now," I said. "Pressing personal business."

"That means there's a girl in the picture," she said.

"Yes, a very special one," I answered.

"Okay, look," she said. "Take them bars to the Mel Fisher people down in Key West. They can tell you just what we've got, where to sell them. They might even buy them from you."

"I can do that," I said. "Where will you be?"

"I suppose I'll get this ticker tuned up," she said. "Then I'll come back down here."

"Are you going to be all right by yourself?" I asked.

"That's the thing," she said. "I've always been just fine by myself, but I'm worried, Breeze. Do this for me before I'm gone from this world. Help me set my daughter up real good."

"I'll help," I said. "I'll do what I can. First I go to the Keys. I'll sell these two, find my girl, and come back for you."

"You've got to look for the rest of it," she said.

"I will, but I'll go get you some cash first," I said.

"Marker seventy-five," she said.

"Which seventy-five?"

"Top of Cayo Costa," she said. "Outside Pelican Bay."

"Did you make a waypoint on your GPS?"

"Nope," she said. "I hit the MOB button on my handheld, but it got accidentally erased later on."

"Where do I look from the marker?"

"Here's what I done," she said. "I sat at that marker and took a dead reckoning over to the old quarantine docks. What I found was inside those ballast rocks that sit near the point."

"I know those rocks," I said. "How far inside?"

"Maybe a hundred yards," she said. "About halfway to shore from the marker."

"How deep?"

"Over my head," she said. "Maybe seven or eight feet."

"What was the tide?"

"Shit, I don't know," she said. "I can't remember everything."

"How far from the original spot did you drop the other two bars?"

"Not far," she said. "Maybe fifteen yards, no more than twenty."

"You sure you trust me to do this?" I asked.

"I've got no one else to ask," she said. "My gut tells me you'll do right by me."

"I'll do my best," I promised.

Two

Another mission had fallen into my lap. This had happened to me time and time again. I was a mission magnet. My to-do list was growing. Step one was to avoid the FBI. Step two was to find Holly. Step three was to sell Shirley's gold. Step four would be to hunt for the rest of her sunken treasure. Holly was a master diver. She'd be a great help in this endeavor, assuming she was willing to come with me.

I had to find her first.

Leap of Faith carried me south towards the Keys. It was an easy run down the coastline. The Ten Thousand Islands slipped by on my port side. I spent one miserable, mosquito ridden night in the Little Shark River. I half expected my old foe Rabble to come knocking, but that didn't happen. I'd chased him down after he stole money from Holly. She'd been all the way down in the Exumas when he ripped her off. I followed his trail and my intuition there to Little Shark. I'd gotten the money back and left him tied up loosely. I assumed he'd manage to free himself, but I wasn't about to go up the river to find his corpse.

The next morning I dodged the lobster traps in Florida Bay and made my way to Boot Key Harbor. During the trip, I heard the Coast Guard hailing me every half hour.

"*Leap of Faith*, *Leap of Faith*, this is the United States Coast Guard, sector Saint Petersburg, Florida hailing. Please respond."

I did not respond. Apparently, the FBI or local law enforcement had enlisted the help of the Coast Guard. That was the last thing I needed. It would be impossible to run from planes and helicopters. It would be hard to hide from them as well.

After I cleared the Seven Mile Bridge, the Coast Guard's message changed. Now I was the subject of a BOLO.

"This is the United States Coast Guard sector Saint Petersburg Florida. All mariners are asked to be on the lookout for a thirty-six-foot power vessel by the name of *Leap of Faith*. White hull with blue canvas believed to be traveling on the west coast of Florida, or possibly the Florida Keys. Mariners are asked to contact the Coast Guard on channel sixteen upon sighting this vessel."

I was about to parade my boat in front of a few hundred liveaboards in Boot Key Harbor. I was known there, to some extent. I doubted many people on the mooring field heard the Coast Guard. Most of them monitored channel sixty-eight, but someone probably heard it. I had to think fast. Boot Key harbor was probably the only place in the Keys where boaters ignored channel sixteen. Anywhere else I might go, other boats would have heard the BOLO. Someone would call me in. I could probably hide amongst the derelicts in Key West, but I wouldn't find Holly hanging out there.

I decided to call Marathon Boatyard. Years back, I'd hired them to refurbish *Leap of Faith*. More recently, they'd done an extensive restoration of Holly's boat, *Another Adventure*. The yard foreman was a gruff old New Englander, but we'd gotten along. I hailed Howie on the VHF.

"Marathon Boat Yard, Marathon Boat Yard. I'm a thirty-six- foot trawler inbound looking for an emergency haul out."

"Is this who I think it is?" came Howie's response. "Take it to seventy-two."

We switched to channel seventy-two.

"It's me," I said. "Don't use my name or my vessel's name."

"What have you done this time?" he asked. "You haven't busted up that old tub again have you?"

"No, she's fine," I said. "I'll explain later. Just haul her out real quick and put her under cover."

"This better be good," he said. "You're interrupting Judge Judy."

"Sorry about that, pal," I said. "I'm just entering your channel now."

"Slow her down, son," he said. "Let me get someone on the lift."

I slowed to a crawl and watched as a man jogged over to the lift. A puff of smoke signaled that he'd started it up. I gave him a minute to get situated. He waved me in and I eased over slings. Two more men arrived to help position things just right. Up went the lift, until I was asked to exit the boat. Howie was waiting for me with crossed arms.

"The good news is that I'm happy to see you," he said. "The bad news is that trouble is likely to follow."

"Did you hear the Coast Guard?" I asked.

"Yep, we all heard them," he answered. "Why are they looking for you?"

"They think I shot a nice lawyer lady over in the Bahamas," I said. "I didn't do it."

"Christ on a cracker," he exclaimed. "You left here with that hot young rasta chick. The two of you went off to who knows where. You come sneaking back in here with this story. What am I going to do with you, Breeze?"

"I hope you'll hide my boat for a bit," I said. "I'll need the name changed. I'll need a canvas person too. All that blue needs to be a different color."

"You want I should repaint the bottom while she's hauled?" he asked. "We can make it red or blue or something."

"Good idea," I said. "Go with red. Tan canvas will work too."

"What are you going to name her?" he asked.

"I don't know yet," I admitted. "I just thought of all this ten minutes ago."

"Flying by the seat of your pants as usual," he said. "I'll get the boys right on it. It's been slow around here."

"Let me get my dinghy down before they move her," I said. "I'll need a way to get around."

"Where you going to sleep?" he asked.

"I haven't figured that out yet either," I answered. "You change the rules about staying onboard here?"

"Still not allowed," he said. "But if you were to slip in here quiet after dark, no one would be the wiser."

"Thanks, Howie," I said. "I appreciate it."

"Keep a low profile, Breeze," he said.

He went off to shout instructions to his crew. I lowered the dinghy and splashed it in the water. I wanted to survey the harbor, look for *Another Adventure*, and get a beer. As I drove the little inflatable around the harbor, I tried to think of another name for my boat. It pained me to change it. According to maritime folklore, it was bad luck to change a boat's name. If you felt compelled to rename it, there was a ceremony you needed to go through to appease the Gods. I'd cross that bridge when I came to it, but I needed to come up with a new name.

I didn't see Holly's boat anywhere. She should have been back in Florida by then, but she could have been anywhere from Miami to Key West. I was certain she'd show up in Marathon eventually. It was all I had to go on now. I couldn't search for her in the dinghy. I made my way to the backside of the harbor, to the Dockside Tropical Café. It was closed. It looked like it had been closed for quite some time. That was disappointing. I swung back west, weaving through the anchored and moored boats until I came to Burdine's Chiki Tiki. It was a good place, but they offered no happy hour specials. Their burgers were always a good choice, though. I grabbed a bar stool and ordered one.

Three beers later I still hadn't thought of a new name for *Leap of Faith*. I think my subconscious was feeling guilty about it. That old boat had gotten me out of a lot of jams. Other women came and went, but she always stuck by me. Changing her name felt like a betrayal, but I didn't have any other choice. She was easy to find. A new name, new canvas, and a new bottom color would give me a fighting chance to elude the FBI or the Coast Guard, or whoever else was looking for *Leap of Faith*.

Two musicians came in and started setting up their gear. I couldn't go back to the boatyard until after dark, so I decided to hang out and listen. I learned later that they were named Cory and Ty. The bar filled up just as they began their first set. They had a loyal local following. They had a nice, easy sound that wasn't quite tropical. There was a country flair to it, even though they sang about islands and rum. They did a good job on some covers of songs I knew. The music helped to take my mind off the trouble I was in. I put five bucks in the tip jar on my way out.

I wondered how Holly was doing, and where she was. I didn't have a phone to try calling her again. If she took the shortest route back to Florida she'd land at Key Biscayne. She was capable of sailing from the Bahamas straight to Marathon, but I doubted she'd chosen that route. She'd been traumatized. She and Jimi had also done some tough sailing to get to the

Bahamas. I speculated that she'd take it easy coming back. All I could do was wait. If she didn't show up, I'd put my boat back in the water and go looking for her.

Sleeping on a boat that is sitting on land is unnatural. I hardly got any rest at all. Howie's crew had covered her up with tarps so there was no air flow. The interior was suffocating. I juggled potential boat names in my mind for hours. I liked the idea of putting my name in it somehow. *Cool Breeze? Following Breeze? Free Breeze?* Then I wondered if the FBI would put two and two together. I dropped that idea.

I briefly considered something that had to do with gold or treasure, but soon ditched that idea too. If I were looking for treasure, there was no point in advertising it to other boats in the area. What was it that mattered the most to me, besides my boat? I pondered what I wanted out of life. I thought about all the choices I'd made that had led up to that very moment. There was one thing that I cherished above all else. Freedom. I'd name the boat *Freedom.*

I found Howie in his office the next day and gave him the news.

"Pretty common name," he said. "But it fits."

"How are the plans coming?" I asked.

"Canvas people will be here today to measure and give me a quote," he said. "What's your money situation? I never know with you."

"I'm good," I told him. "Cost doesn't really matter. Just don't let them rip me off."

"We'll sand the bottom before they get started with the new canvas," he said. "We'll paint it after they're done."

"And the new name?" I asked.

"That will be last," he said. "You'll have to do it right. Bring the champagne. Do the little speech and whatnot."

"I knew you'd think that way," I said.

"No point in angering the Gods," he said. "Believe in superstition or not."

"I hear you," I said. "I'll do it right."

"Okay, now get out of my hair," he said. "Some of us still have to work for a living."

I took another dinghy ride around the harbor. There was no sign of Holly or her boat. I decided to go out Sister's Creek to Sombrero Beach. She hadn't anchored anywhere along the way. I stood in the sand and looked out over the ocean. There was a distant sailboat, riding the breeze. I watched it for twenty minutes. It didn't come in towards Boot Key Harbor.

That night I tried hailing her on the VHF radio. I didn't use my boat name. I just called for *Another Adventure*, over and over again. There was no reply. I tried channel sixteen. I also tried channel seventy-two. That was the channel we used to communicate when we were together. She didn't answer either channel. I sat under the tarps, sweating and sipping rum.

Where are you, Holly?

Three

Three days went by. Each morning I made the rounds in the dinghy. Each afternoon I drank beer at Burdine's, waiting for dark. Each night, I drank enough rum to help me sleep. The canvas had been stripped from the bridge. The bottom had been sanded bare. There was dust all over everything. *Leap of Faith* was looking rough. I reminded her that in order to make a cake you had to break a few eggs. She wasn't happy about being on the hard. Her name had been removed. She was really pissed off about that. I promised to make it right, someday.

I'd put her through worse misery in our time together. I hit something offshore and busted up her running gear. That's how I'd met Howie and his crew. She'd been riddled full of bullet holes after that. I worked tirelessly to repair all the damage, but the holes were still evident if you looked hard enough. She'd almost sunk more than once. A busted hose over in the Bahamas had been repaired on the fly. A cut hose in Florida by some asshole who wanted revenge on me had almost done her in for good. This episode wasn't nearly so bad, except for the name change. She wasn't mad at the bottom job or the canvas work. She was mad about the name change. I couldn't blame her.

On the fourth day, I saw her coming in. I was sitting up at Burdine's. *Another Adventure* came gliding by, sails up, no motor running. I moved to the railing and yelled out to her.

"Holly, look up," I said, waving my arms.

"Breeze!" she yelled back. "Follow me in."

I tossed a twenty on the bar and ran down the steps. I untied the dinghy and started after her. I caught up just as she went through the Bridge to Nowhere. She veered off the channel in an area filled with derelicts. Her mainsail came down. She continued east a few hundred more yards into a slightly better neighborhood. The jib came down. Her boat glided along, slowing. Finally, I watched Holly move forward and slide an anchor over. She went back to the cockpit, started the engine, and backed down on her ground tackle. I pulled alongside just as she got settled in.

"Jesus, Breeze," she said. I'm so glad to see you."

"You'll be even happier in a minute," I said. "I've got news."

"I've been so worried," she said. "What's the deal?"

"No one is looking for you," I told her. "Not the cops, not the FBI, not anybody. You're free to move about freely."

"How can that be possible?" she asked.

"Taylor is alive," I said. "She accused me. I'm a fugitive again."

"That's awful," she said. "We've got to do something."

"Do what?" I asked. "We can't tell them you pulled the trigger. If one of us has to be on the run, let it be me."

"I feel terrible," she said. "I can turn myself in, explain what happened."

"You'll do no such thing," I scolded. "I can handle it."

"But you're right here in the open," she said. "They'll see your boat for sure."

"It's under cover over at the boatyard," I told her. "Soon to have new colors and a new name."

"I can't believe you're changing her name," she said.

"Me neither," I said. "But it's got to be done."

"Then what?" she asked. "You'll just run forever?"

"Only until they stop looking," I said. "Give it a couple months and I'll be forgotten."

"What do you want to do in the meantime?" she asked.

"First we go to Key West," I said.

"Just like every crook that ever went on the run," she said. "Seems kind of hokey, doesn't it?"

I told her all about Shirley's gold. Her eyes lit up when I mentioned the two lost bars and the potential for more. She didn't know that area very well, but she was a far superior diver to me. We'd make a good team.

"A treasure hunt," she said. "You never cease to amaze me. I can't believe you're giving me gold fever."

"I know, I know. Every fool in Florida wants to find gold," I said. "But Shirley gave me two examples. They're real. I can assure you."

"So we sell those two, give the money to Shirley, and go look for the rest of it. That's our plan?"

"That's the plan," I said. "FBI be damned."

"I assume we'll be taking my boat?" she asked.

"Makes sense," I answered. "No one looking for me knows your boat."

"I hate anchoring in Key West," she said.

"We'll take the bus down," I said. "Do our deal, then come back and sail back north."

"Can a girl take a shower first?" she said, laughing. "I might need a day to digest all of this."

"Of course," I replied. "Think you could sneak me in? I've got no access to the showers where my boat is."

"We can do a two-for-one if you're game," she suggested. "Saves water."

"Sign me up," I answered.

We took my dinghy up to Marathon City Marina. Neither of us had a key card to get in. We waited until someone came out and grabbed the door before it closed. We started to wash, but our need to be clean was overridden by our need to have sex. It was purely a physical desire, with no coy remarks or foreplay. We just went at it like animals. When she groaned I stuck my hand over her mouth and picked up the pace. It was over pretty quick for both of us. We stood there in silence, just holding on. The water ran over us. Finally, she broke the silence.

"That was different," she whispered.

"Was it good?" I asked.

"Damn good," she replied. "Now let's wash up."

Afterward, we walked across the street to the Lobster House. We sat in the corner by ourselves so we could talk. A lot had happened over the past few weeks. I sensed she wanted to sort some of it out.

"Are you okay?" I asked. "I'm really sorry about how that whole thing went down. I hope you understand why I had to send you away."

"I get it now," she said. "You were looking out for me. I was just rattled."

"I'm extremely grateful for what you did for me," I said. "I could have very easily been the one with a bullet in me."

"Your plan didn't turn out so hot," she said. "You underestimated how evil Taylor was."

"I can't argue with that," I said. "Hopefully, her evil ass will rot in jail for a very long time."

"Tell me you're done with your battle of the wills with her," she said. "Just let it go."

"She's locked up," I said. "There's nothing else I can do. It's over."

"Can I tell you the truth about something?" she asked.

"Of course."

"When I pulled the trigger, I wanted her dead," she admitted. "She was living rent-free in your head. She was so damn pretty. I hated her. Damn good shot too. I couldn't let her shoot you."

"I think your psyche might be better off with her alive," I said.

"Oh, I agree," she said. "As soon as I saw her go down I got scared. I'm not really a killer."

"Are you sure you're going to be all right?" I asked.

"I'm sure," she answered. "You did the right thing keeping her alive. You did the right thing for me by sending me away. The plan didn't quite work, but you were true to me. True Breeze."

"I'll try to avoid the need for gunfire in the future," I said.

"What about our future?" she asked. "We run into each other by chance and now it's just like the old times?"

"Hell, I hadn't thought about it," I said. "Just going with the flow."

"Your flow takes you towards trouble more often than not," she said. "I don't know if I want that all the time. I was shitting my pants over there in the Bahamas. It was crazy what we were doing."

"It doesn't always have to be crazy," I said.

"I hope not. I can't just stay cool and collected like you when the shit hits the fan. The adrenaline is going to give me a heart attack. How do you do it?"

"It's a gift I guess," I said. "I've thought over the possible outcomes. Things slow down for me. I just do what has to be done."

"Is this gold thing going to blow up in our faces?" she asked.

"I can't see how," I said. "Seems harmless enough. There are no other players except Shirley. She's in her eighties."

Back at Holly's boat, we continued briefly.

"Okay," she said. "Let's go to Key West in the morning. Where are you sleeping?"

"I sneak back into the boatyard after dark."

"Can you do that again?" she asked. "I'm thrilled that we caught up with each other, but I really need to clear my head after today."

"No problem," I said, secretly disappointed.

"Thanks, Breeze," she said. "I mean it. Thanks for everything, shower included."

"Rest up," I said. "Tomorrow we make a shady gold deal on the mean streets of Key Weird."

"This better not turn weird," she said. "I've had enough excitement."

"Good night, Holly," I said. "Sweet dreams."

"Sweet dreams to you too, asshole," she said with a chuckle.

Four

I spent another night in dust and sweat under the tarps. I was feeling good about things. I'd reunited with Holly. I'd gotten laid. I'd even gotten a shower out of the deal. All in all, it was a pretty good day. A new mission was about to begin. As far as I knew, the FBI was losing my scent. Sometimes it paid to be off the grid. I lay in the bunk and fantasized about what I'd do with a million dollars.

It had long been my dream to live out my days with a beautiful woman on some tropical island. Holly and I had possibilities once, but her dream was to sail the seven seas. She was rethinking that dream these days. Maybe we could try again. Take our millions and lose ourselves in paradise. Maybe if I promised her no more missions, I could convince her to go with me. It was pleasant to think about.

The reality was something different. Shirley was a half-addled dreamer. She'd had the gold bug for decades. Her story might be a bunch of bull. She just needed me to sell those bars for her. The rest of the story was to give me the incentive to help her. Holly was twenty years younger than me. She was attractive in a hippie girl sort of way. She was fresh faced and bright eyed when I'd first met her. Now she was wary of my adventures. I couldn't blame her for that. Our relationship was tough to figure out. I was no father figure, we had sex for crying out loud. I was somewhat of a mentor, though. We didn't use the words of lovers, but we clearly cared for one another. She wasn't ready to resign her love to such an older man. I was slow to open up and give completely, but so was she.

She'd been hurt by young fools who didn't know what a treasure she was. I'd been hurt by loss. Our current lot in life was to help each other out. Our future was completely unknown. It was just as likely that she'd take her cut of whatever treasure we found and sail away forever. She probably thought the same of me.

We caught the early bus to Key West. Holly had called the Mel Fisher Museum and made an appointment with the curator. Her name was Susan Pierson. She agreed to evaluate Shirley's gold. As soon as we unwrapped the two bars, her eyes got big. She pushed intercom button and asked for the executive director to come to her office. I took this as a good sign. We had something valuable.

The director was another woman. Her name was Melissa Kendrick. She ignored us and went straight to the gold pieces. She studied them first with the naked eye, then with a tiny telescope-like device.

"Where did you get these?" she asked.

"From a crazy old lady on a sailboat," I responded.

"I mean geographic location," she said. "And your name is?"

"Breeze," I said. "This is Holly."

"Nice to meet you," she said. "Now, where did these come from?"

"Pardon me," I said. "But I don't think I'll tell the world's greatest treasure hunters where they came from if you don't mind."

"I appreciate your caution," she said. "Completely understandable, but you don't realize what you've got here. It may have great historical significance."

"We were hoping to turn them into cash," I said. "The old lady needs the money. They belong to her."

"We don't purchase gold here, Mr. Breeze," she said. "We dig it up off the ocean floor."

"Can you tell me what they're worth?" I asked.

"They could be weighed and checked for composition and purity," she said. "But they could be worth much more as historical artifacts. I strongly oppose selling it for its gold value alone."

"What makes you think they have some special value?" I asked. "Just looks like hunks of gold to me."

"What you have here," she began. "Is an example of what the early Spanish conquerors did with Aztec gold. They melted down figurines, idols, statues and such, for easier transport."

"How can you tell?" I asked.

"The faint reddish tint in the gold are most likely copper," she explained. "The Aztecs used copper for adornments on their objects. Eyes, jewelry, headdress or whatever, were made out of copper. The Spaniards simply melted the entire object, rendering it less than pure."

"So how old are we talking?"

"Sixteen hundred. After that, they started mining their own gold. It was all marked with weight and ownership details," she said. "Knowing where you found this would help with further research."

"Let's just say on the west coast of Florida," I offered.

"The Spanish didn't carry gold up the west coast," she said. "At least not on purpose. That would suggest pirates."

"There's plenty of folklore about west coast pirates," I said. "Gasparilla most notably."

"Most of which is nonsense," she said. "No significant finds have been made to support the wives tales told about Jose Gaspar."

"There's two bars of gold sitting right in front of you," I pointed out. "Which you say may have significant historical value. Susan here lit up like a Roman candle when she first laid eyes on them."

"The museum would offer you a contract, pay an upfront fee or a percentage or a combination of the two if you'll pinpoint the location of this find."

"I don't think so," I said.

"Can I assume that you think there is more where these were found?" she asked.

"I told you," I said. "I didn't find them. The old lady who did says there at least two more."

"Will you be attempting to retrieve them," she asked. "And look around for more?"

"Look, if I can't turn these two into cash, then finding more doesn't make much sense," I said. "How do I go about getting paid?"

"Any gold buyer will take them for pennies on the dollar," she said. "It would be a shame, though."

"What are they worth in gold value alone?" I asked.

She put each bar on a scale and examined them further.

"One is just under ten ounces," she said. "The other is just over ten ounces."

"What's that mean in American dollars?" I asked.

"Credit Suisse or Perth Mint gold bars that are ninety-nine point nine percent pure are going at a little over thirteen hundred dollars," she said. "These aren't pure, and they have no markings. They can only be melted down into something else. Cheap jewelry likely."

"Ten grand each?" I asked.

"We won't buy them," she said. "Others probably will, but please don't do that."

"What would you have me do, Miss Kendrick?" I asked. "My friend can't eat gold bars."

"Work with us," she said. "There is no finer team in the field. We find more of these, but we also look for intact figures. If we find idols or statues we can definitively identify the source. You would be a rich man."

"I'm not concerned with being rich," I said. "But my friend needs help. She can't wait for some long expedition to find the mother lode. She's in poor health."

"Then find the mother lode yourself," she said. "But I must warn you about something. Almost all trade in this sort of thing is illegal. The state of Florida wants its cut. Museums don't have the funds to make multi-million dollar purchases. It's a dark underground world. People often turn up dead."

Holly jabbed me with a sharp elbow. The mood in the room got darker. I'd read multiple stories about these little idols. Montezuma's Treasure came to mind. Various legends report huge stores of hidden gold in southwestern America. Any person who has ever tried to locate it has died in the process. Then there was the novel by John D. MacDonald where Travis McGee's buddy gets murdered over his possession of a collection of golden idols from Mexico.

In spite of the ill-wind wafting around the room, I decided to keep the treasure's location to myself.

"If I change my mind about enlisting your help," I said. "I'll get back in touch."

"It would be the wise thing to do," she said.

This woman obviously didn't know me, or my long history of less than wise decisions. I had to go my own way. It's just who I was. I can perfectly understand how the average person would be happy to turn over the search to professionals. They'd be happy with whatever small cut they received. I saw it as Shirley's gold, and she'd asked me to recover it. She could have sold the location to the Mel Fisher people if she wanted to. She might be a little batty but she wasn't stupid.

We walked out of the Mel Fisher Museum, still carrying the gold bars.

"What are we going to do now?" Holly asked.

"Go find the rest of it," I answered.

"What about Shirley's money?" she asked.

"I've got cash back on the boat," I said. "I'll give her the twenty grand we could have gotten for selling them."

"Are you going to tell her the whole story?" she asked.

"I guess so," I said. "It's her find."

"And you get half?"

"We get half," I said. "Assuming you're in."

"I didn't appreciate the comment that lady made about people turning up dead," she said.

"We don't have anything to get killed over," I said. "Let's worry about finding something first. We'll deal with the rest of it later."

"That's my Breeze," she said. "Half-assed but full speed."

"Damn the torpedoes," I replied. "Are you in?"

"Yea, I'm in."

We rode the bus back to Marathon. Holly didn't drink anymore so there was no point in hanging out in Key West. From the dinghy dock, we went straight to the boatyard. It didn't look like any progress had been made on my boat. Howie said he was still waiting on the canvas people. I climbed aboard and retrieved a coffee can full of cash from its hiding place. We went back out to Holly's boat to work on a plan.

"We don't know shit about this," Holly said. "We're not prepared in the slightest."

"We know where to look," I countered. "We'll figure something out."

"That's your answer to everything," she said. "I'll figure something out."

"Except this time I said we. We're a team on this."

"So how do we start?" she asked.

"We take your boat up to Goodland," I started. "We visit with Shirley, get any details she may have left out. Pay her, and go diving the area she gave me."

"I've got two hookah rigs," she said. "It will go faster if we both look."

"I thought someone was always supposed to stay above," I said. "In case something went wrong."

"Now you're worried about safety?" she asked.

"There may be sharks to look out for," I suggested.

"This just keeps getting better," she said. "Sharks, dead people. You sort of promised me that this would be a cake walk."

"It still may be," I said. "Make a few dives. Bring up some gold. Figure out how to sell it."

"How do you maintain such optimism?" she asked. "Your history suggests that this will go off the rails somewhere along the way."

"My history suggests that I'm quite capable of overcoming whatever SNAFU may present itself."

"Until your luck runs out," she said.

"So far, so good," I responded.

We stopped at Pancho's marina the next day to fill up with fuel and water. We decided not to enter Little Shark River. Instead, we sailed through the night, arriving in Goodland the next morning. The approach to Coon Key was shallow for *Another Adventure*, but we managed to crawl up the river until we got to town. We anchored in the deepest part of the harbor, barely outside the channel markers. Shirley's boat was back where I'd seen her previously.

We hopped in the dinghy to pay her a visit. We found her with a can of Rustoleum in one hand and a paintbrush in the other. She had specks of white paint in her hair and on her bathing suit. She was busy repainting the topsides of her boat when we pulled alongside.

"What the hell you doing, Shirl?" I asked.

"I don't want them to find me dead with a dirty looking boat," she said.

"You could have tried cleaning it first," I suggested.

"Don't want to waste the water," she said. "Rustoleum covers up everything."

She was slopping paint right over the top of dust and dried bugs. The canvas on her bimini top had torn apart. She'd used fishing line to sew it back to the frame. Another paint brush sat in a coffee cup full of gasoline. She was an unconventional coot, but she managed to survive. She just made do with what she had.

"Did you get your pacemaker adjusted?" I asked.

"Did you sell my gold?" she asked back.

"You first," I said.

"I went to the doctor," she said. "He turned it up a few notches for me. Then he scolded me about rum and cigarettes and hard living."

"You can buy all the rum and cigarettes you want now," I said.

"You got money for them bars?" she asked. "Because the hard living ain't worth it without rum and cigarettes."

"I've got money for you," I said. "We need to talk it over, though."

"How much?"

"Twenty grand."

"Hot damn!" She yipped. "Let's go to the bar."

"We shouldn't talk in public," I said. "That's how you discovered the gold in the first place. Tourists talking in a bar."

"Well you can't sit here," she said. "I've done painted every place you might sit on."

"Grab some shorts and a shirt," I said. "We'll talk on the way in."

When Shirley climbed down into the dinghy, she left white footprints on it. The bottoms of her feet were both white with paint. We took her to *Another Adventure* where Holly helped her get the paint off. It took some acetone and a stiff brush to get her cleaned up. She cussed the whole time. I explained to her what we'd learned in Key West. I told her what we planned to do. I waited while she thought it over.

"Well, I've been feeling a little better since I got this ticker tuned up," she said. "I reckon I'll live a while longer."

"What about your daughter?" I asked. "Is this money enough?"

"I had ideas on making her rich," she said. "Go and find the rest of the gold, Breeze."

That was a good enough blessing for me. We dropped the gold talk and went into the bar. It was called the Little Bar. It was a low-key little shack of a place with a huge menu that hung tableside. Shirl said it had the least number of tourists out of our limited options in Goodland. I doubted it was a place that the FBI would visit. I got Shirley a rum and coke. I got myself a beer. I got Holly a rum punch with no rum in it. We repeated our order three times before Shirl got drunk enough to slur her speech.

Back at Shirley's little boat, we helped her climb up and over the safety lines. She sat down and immediately regretted it. The paint hadn't completely dried. She stood up to reveal a newly painted butt. She dropped her shorts right there in the cockpit. There was nothing underneath. We got waved away.

"Nobody wants to see an old woman's ass," she said. "Go on. Find that gold."

Five

When Holly and I first met, I knew nothing about sailing. By now, I'd spent enough time on *Another Adventure* to learn the basics. Holly was a pure sailor. She loved nothing more than to harness the power of the wind. She wanted to go offshore and sail all night to Cayo Costa. She was the captain aboard her vessel, so I had to agree.

We had to decide what to do about the Cape Romano Shoals. Goodland was tucked up well under the Cape. To avoid the shoals we'd have to back-track south, then turn west to go around them. To cross directly over the shoals, we'd have to zig and zag, keeping a constant eye on the depth finder. It would be tedious, but it would cut twenty miles off our trip. Holly chose to go through them. I was on chart and depth finder duty while she tended the sails.

We picked our way carefully through and popped out of the shoals below Marco Island. After that, it was an easy reach up the Gulf to the Boca Grande Pass. We each got plenty of rest. There were no obstacles to avoid other than stone crab traps. The wind wasn't strong, but it was enough to keep us gliding along at six knots. We made the Pass just after sunrise. I wanted to go into Pelican Bay to drop anchor. Holly was afraid of the shallows. Her vessel's six-foot draft was a handicap, but I assured her it was doable.

"I've done this a hundred times," I told her. "Just take it nice and slow. I'll guide us in."

"If we run aground, it's on you," she warned.

"We'll be fine," I said. "Just pay attention to what I tell you."

"What's the tide?" she asked.

"Doesn't matter," I told her. "Everything is at least six feet even at dead low."

"I draw six feet," she said.

"We'll anchor in ten," I said. "If that makes you happy."

"You're the expert," she said.

"Well, yes," I said. "When it comes to Pelican Bay, I am an expert. This is my home."

"I defer to your greater experience," she said. "You want to take the wheel?"

"Not under sail," I said. "You're the expert there."

Holly steered and I guided. We slid through the narrow entrance without touching bottom. We continued past the park service docks through seven-foot depths. We found the ten-foot hole, stopped and dropped anchor.

"Easy peasy," I said, stealing a line from Shirley.

"Show me on the chart where this gold is," Holly said.

"Here," I said, pointing to marker seventy-five. "We passed it on the way in."

"Why didn't we just anchor out there?" she asked.

"We've got more protection in here," I said. "I like it in here. No point in announcing to the world that we're on a treasure hunt. We can just take the dinghy out there and poke around. Act like snorkelers."

"I still think it would be easier to have the big boat nearby," she said.

"If we start hauling up busloads of gold, we can always move closer," I said.

"You really think there're busloads of gold down there?"

"I've got no idea," I said. "That's why we just check it out first. Try to find the two bars Shirley dropped."

"Worst comes to worst, we'll have twenty grand," she said.

"Shirley gets half," I reminded her. "We each get five grand."

"That's not much," she said.

"It's a start," I said. "What we really want is one of those little idols."

"Which is worth millions," she said. "If we can sell it."

"Exactly," I said. "That's what you call incentive."

We loaded the dive gear into the dinghy and drove it back out to the spot Shirley had told me about. I went straight for marker seventy-five, only to find several boats fishing in our target area. I did not want to dive in clear sight of them. They were probably fishing the high tide for sheepshead. I always saw them near the ballast rocks off the quarantine docks. We'd have to come back when there were no fishermen nearby.

We turned around and went back. Instead of returning to the boat, I stopped on the sand bar just inside the entrance. Two other boats were beached nearby. A dog was running back and forth, barking at bait fish. I pulled the dinghy up onto dry sand so it wouldn't float away. We walked around the point until we could see the marker and the anchored fishing boats. They were still there.

We went back to Holly's boat disappointed. I hadn't considered that folks would be anchored there, though I'd seen them fishing that spot in the past. We'd have to try again in the morning.

"You know we are totally half-assing this thing, right?" said Holly.

"What else are we supposed to do?" I asked.

"Didn't you read how Mel Fisher found the Atocha?" she asked.

"Mel Fisher didn't have the damn near exact coordinates," I answered.

"Granted," she said. "But still, we could find this stuff easily with the right equipment, assuming it's there."

"So what do we need?"

"Underwater metal detector would be nice," she said.

"How do we get one of those?

"Couldn't tell you," she said. "I doubt the local Ace Hardware carries them."

"What about a regular metal detector?" I asked. "Do you think it would read down through the water?"

"Probably not as deep as we need it to," she said.

"Google it on your phone," I said.

"Good idea."

Holly spent a few minutes with her phone, clicking links and reading. As I waited, I renewed the argument about getting a phone for myself. The ability to search Google, or maps, or even to communicate with the rest of the world, would be nice. My problem was justified paranoia. I knew that government agencies could track you through your phone, especially the FBI. If they wanted to find me, they'd do it through my phone. That possibility was reason enough not to get one.

"Here we go," said Holly. "There's a variety of underwater detectors on the market."

"How do we get one?

"Looks like Amazon is the best bet," she said.

"I don't have a credit card," I said. "Or a place to ship to."

"I have a debit card," she said. "But not much money in the bank. I keep cash now, just like you."

"I could give you the money," I said. "You deposit it. We buy the detector. We need a shipping address."

"If you pick up a mooring ball in Boot Key, they will accept packages for you."

"We just left Boot Key," I said.

"That's all I've got," she said. "My bank is in Marathon. We can get a package delivered to the city marina."

"If we can't find anything, we'll go that route," I said. "Let's dive it first."

"I'm antsy to take a look around," she admitted.

We went back to the site the next morning. We saw no fishing boats. I lined up marker seventy-five with the point by the quarantine docks. I guessed at the distance, stopping half-way between the two marks. I dropped an over-sized anchor down into the sand. Holly fired up the dive rig. She wore flippers and a mask. She didn't need a wetsuit in the warm water. Water clarity was not good. The current was strong. She stuck her face in the water for a few seconds.

"I can see about two feet," she said. "Why is it so brown?"

"Tannin from the rivers, mostly," I said. "But we're getting some of the lake discharges through Pine Island Sound."

"I'm ready to go down," she said. "Yank the air hose if I need to come up quick."

I gave her a thumbs up as she went under. She carried a thin rope, which she attached to the anchor. She planned to swim increasingly larger circles away from the anchor until she ran out of rope. I couldn't see the bottom. She disappeared from sight on her way down. I scanned the area. I saw no one approaching us. I saw no shark fins slicing the surface. Bubbles came up from Holly's breather.

It took her twenty minutes to cover the circle. She had twenty foot of rope out, which meant the circle was forty feet in diameter. She found nothing. We moved forty feet closer to shore and repeated the process. I made a waypoint at each spot on my handheld GPS. She dove for another twenty minutes with no success.

"I don't know how many dives I can take," she said. "The current is kicking my ass."

"Rest for a few minutes," I said. "Get a drink."

I moved us another forty feet. Shirley's dead reckoning was a bit off. Either that or she was full of shit. When Holly came up empty on the third dive, we moved back out to where we started. I positioned us forty feet further away from shore. Holly went down again. She came up with nothing. We moved another forty feet out and she went under for the fifth time.

The fifth time was the charm. Her hand broke the surface holding a slab of gold just like the bars Shirley had given me. Her face came out of the water sporting a big smile. She yipped and yahooed, waving both hands and doing a little water dance. I helped her back aboard and we both danced a little jig.

"I think I saw the other one," she said. "But I got all excited. I had to bring this one up."

"You up for going back down for it?" I asked.

"I've got one more dive left in me," she said. "I'm whooped, but I can get the other one."

After a break, she went after it. She was only gone a few minutes. She came up with the second bar. She looked beat. Two boats were headed our way. The sheepshead bite must have still been good. We packed up our gear and left before they dropped anchor.

Back aboard *Another Adventure* Holly stripped down and rinsed off with fresh water. Seeing her naked body out on deck was always a treat. She was young and fit. She had ripped abs and curves in the right places. She had no idea how attractive she was. She'd spent too much time playing the tomboy and turning wrenches. She never wore makeup. Her hair was generally a mess. I didn't care. I thought she was pretty.

"So what now?" she asked, covering herself with a towel.

"Those two are all we know about for sure," I said. "Shirley didn't say she saw more."

"Hard to believe that there're just four random bars laying in the sand down there," she said.

"I agree, but it's just a blind search now," I said.

"Let me try another day, near where we left off," she suggested. "If we can't find anything, we get us a detector."

"Sounds reasonable," I said. "What else could we use to search?"

"Those pieces I found today were just under the sand," she said. "I could barely make out the outline in the poor visibility."

"A light?" I asked.

"I was thinking more of a way to blow the sand away," she said.

"Use the prop like Mel Fisher?" I asked.

We both moved to the stern and looked down at the back of the boat. She had no swim platform or any other structure to fasten the gear to. Neither of us could figure out a way to attach anything that would direct the force of the prop downward.

"I could do it with my boat," I said. "I've got a platform with a bunch of brackets under it. I've got a bigger prop. It could be done."

"You sure you want to risk bringing it up here?" she asked.

"It should be ready to go by the time we get back," I said. "New paint, new name, new canvas."

"We could get the metal detector shipped," she offered.

"Then we come back and clean the place out," I said. "Shouldn't take long if we get it rigged right."

"This is fun," she said. "Searching for a sunken treasure on high seas. We be pirates, bitches."

After six fruitless dives the next day, it was no longer fun. The current was playing havoc with Holly's searches. The turbid water was impossible to see through. She had resorted to feeling along the bottom with her hands. We started to wonder if there was any more to find. Other than the ballast rocks, the bottom was flat and featureless. Discouragement overtook enthusiasm and we called off the search.

"Looks like we're going back to Marathon," I said.

"I'm tired, but I haven't given up," she said. "We'll put some resources on this place and find something. I can feel it."

"Now who's the optimist?" I asked.

"It's your fault," she said. "You infected me with the gold fever."

"Like I said, those four bars were all we had to go on," I said. "Might not be anything else down there."

"It's there," she said. "We just found a piece of it. Let's get our shit in order. Do it right. Make ourselves rich and famous."

"The last thing I need is to be famous," I said. "I don't even need the money. I just wanted to help Shirley."

"You're welcome to give me your share," she said, laughing. "The FBI isn't looking for me."

"Gee, thanks, pal," I said. "Just looking out for my best interest, right?"

"Speaking of that," she began. "What if we do make some huge find of international importance? How are you going to deal with that, without getting caught?"

"I don't know," I said. "I guess you'll have to be the face of the organization. I'll hide in the background, waiting for you to return with big bags of cash."

"We can both take a bath in hundred dollar bills," she said. "Walk around smelling like money."

"Beats how you smell right now," I said. "You need another shower."

"You always know how to make a girl feel special," she said. "But you're right. The water stinks."

"You should wear a wetsuit and hood from now on," I suggested. "Take care of any cuts or scrapes right away."

"You're welcome to take a shift down there anytime," she said.

"You're so much better at it," I said. "I'd just slow us down."

"What is it you do for this outfit?" she asked.

"Other than being chief cook and bottle washer," I said. "I gleaned this location from my extensive connections in the gold recovery underground of Goodland."

"So your contribution is knowing Shirley," she said. "And you admit that she's a bit goofy."

"I cultivated my relationship with my confidential informant with years of rum and cigarette donations," I said. "That ought to be worth something."

"Oh, you're something all right," she said. "I'm just not sure what."

"When we come back," I said. "I'll be the captain of a treasure recovery vessel."

"Let's hope so," she said. "Otherwise this is all a big waste of time."

"What else have you got to do?"

"Nothing, I guess," she admitted. "Plus, the company's not bad."

"Likewise, fair maiden," I said. "Now, let's secure all this crap. Make ready to sail in the morning."

Six

The next morning, I was down below when Holly warned me to stay down. The FWC was approaching. They came alongside but didn't raft up to us.

"Good morning, ma'am," the officer said. "Have you seen a trawler named *Leap of Faith* here lately?"

"No sir," she answered. "But I've only been here a few days. Heading south today."

"Going to the Keys?" he asked.

"I've got friends in Marathon," she said.

"If you happen to run across that trawler, we ask that you contact the Coast Guard," he said.

"Sure, no problem," she said.

"Have a nice trip," the officer said, as he pulled away.

The bad news was that another agency had been enlisted in the search for me. The good news was that they were looking for *Leap of Faith*. I wasn't aboard that vessel. By the time I was, she'd have a different name. We both shrugged and prepared to raise the anchor.

Holly sailed us south without incident. We took advantage of steady east winds to fly down the coast. I was becoming accustomed to being underway without a motor running. Whenever I traveled on *Leap of Faith*, I had the drone of the diesel to accompany me. It was comforting to hear the old engine purring along. Any change in her tone alerted me to problems.

Cruising on *Another Adventure* was quite different. The water sloshing along her hull and the occasional flap of a sail were all the sound we heard. The big sailboat was an extension of Holly. She was one with it. She could read clues in her lean. She could read the wind in her telltales. She could gauge her speed by the way she sliced through the sea. When I was driving my own boat, I was constantly checking gauges for oil pressure, and engine temperature. That wasn't necessary on a boat under sail.

I took my shifts at the helm and tried to learn the feel of her. I'd improved as a sailor. I could be of some use to Holly now, but I'd never become a full-time blow boater. I was trawler trash through and through. That would never change.

"Now is a good time to take a step back and reassess this mission," Holly said.

"You want to cash out what we have and call it quits?" I asked her.

"I don't know, just thinking out loud," she said. "We've got four bars worth forty grand in gold value alone. Shirley gets twenty. We each get ten. Not a bad day's work."

"I'm willing to drop a thousand bucks on the metal detector," I said. "Plus a little more to rig up something to use the prop wash. I think it's worth a shot."

"All so Shirley can give the money to someone you've never even met?"

"Shirley asked me to help," I said. "I agreed to help. That's pretty much all there is to it."

"You asked me to help, and I agreed."

"So I guess we're still looking for gold," I said.

"Guess so."

In Marathon, we picked up a mooring ball. We needed to be official customers in order to receive packages. That also would give us legal access to the showers, and free Wi-Fi in the dayroom. I paid for a week's stay. Holly used her IPad to get online and shop for underwater metal detectors. I went to the boatyard to check on things.

The tarps had been removed. The faded blue canvas had been replaced with crisp new tan canvas. The flaking black bottom paint had been replaced with bright new red paint. Across her stern, the name *Freedom* glistened in the afternoon sun. Howie stood next to her with his arms crossed.

"We had to use some solvent to get the old name off," he said. "So I had the transom waxed real good after the new name went on. Looked so good I had them wax the whole boat. Pretty ain't she?"

"Nice work, as usual," I said. "Now comes the part when you rob me of my last penny."

"You said you were good for it," he said. "I didn't even ask for any money up front. You being a good repeat customer and all."

"I'm good for it," I said. "Just trying to limit how bad you cheat me."

"Good work comes at a price," he said. "You know that. Not to mention hiding her for you with no questions asked."

"Good point," I admitted. "Let's go settle up."

After I paid the bill, which was indeed too much, I asked about some additional work. I told Howie what I was trying to do. I wanted a way to rig up a tube that would direct the prop wash down towards the bottom. The wash would blow the sand away from the bottom, revealing whatever was buried beneath it. He understood what I wanted. He was also curious. I pled with him to keep the work secret.

"You leave here with that rig, half the boats in the harbor will follow you," he said. "One of these boys will talk anyway. Word moves fast on this island."

"Make it removable," I said. "Something that I can assemble on site."

"I can run braces down from your swim platform brackets," he said. "But how are you going to attach the tube under water?"

"I'll have help," I said. "Better diver than me."

"Can they turn wrenches down under?" he asked.

"Better than me," I assured him. "Wrench turner from way back."

"Not like you to take on a partner," he said. "Especially if you're up to what I think you are."

"You've met her," I said. "Cute blond with dreads."

"I would have guessed you'd have run her off a long time ago," he said. "You old sea dog."

"We go back and forth," I said.

"I bet you do," he said. "I'm going to need a few days to put your rig together."

"No problem," I said. "We're here for a week."

"Keep quiet down here, Breeze," he said. "Some of these dirt bags will cut your throat just to know where you're looking."

"I should probably sneak out in the dark," I said. "The site is pretty far from here. Not in the Keys."

"I don't want to know," he said. "Come back in three days. We'll arrange to splash your boat when you're ready to leave."

"Thanks again, Howie."

I found Holly taking notes and scrolling through Amazon on her IPad. She had narrowed the choices to two. Both sold for fifteen hundred dollars.

"I know it's more than we thought," she said. "But these two are the best technology out there."

"How do we decide which one to get?"

"The Minelab Excalibur II has a lithium battery, but the reviews aren't that great," she explained.

"What's the other one?"

"The Fisher CZ21-8," she said. "All good reviews. Simple to use."

"They both cost the same?"

"Exactly the same."

"Let's go with the Fisher," I said. "You know, like in Mel Fisher."

"I like it," she said. "We'll have to get to the bank and make a deposit before I can order it."

"Let's roll then."

It took two days for her deposit to be available. She ordered the detector and had it shipped to Marathon City Marina. I went back to take a look at the rig Howie had designed. It was rudimentary, but I didn't see why it wouldn't work. Two backing plates bolted together formed clamps on either side of the swim platform. They had a hole for another bolt that held the long aluminum arms extending down to either side of the prop. The tube was fashioned out of a plastic drum. The bottom had been cut out and smaller backing plates had been fastened to both sides. It bolted up nicely to the aluminum arms. Its angle could be adjusted by loosening bolts and tilting it up or down. The entire thing was light weight and easy to break down and assemble.

"I used aluminum to keep the weight down," said Howie. "Same with the plastic drum. Neither will be bothered by saltwater."

"It's almost like you've made something like this before," I said.

"I've got a general idea," he said. "Everybody knows how Mel Fisher used to do it."

"It's pretty old school," I said. "But it should work for our purposes."

"Just be real careful with it," he said. "Be mindful of your hands and feet when that prop is turning."

"What do I owe you?"

"Bring me back a nice gold necklace," he said.

"So far we've only found rough bars," I told him.

"That'll work."

We arranged to put *Freedom* in the water in two days. The launch would be during the daylight, but she'd be parked for an easy exit when I came for her after dark. We'd have the detector by then. We also needed to take care of necessary chores like provisioning. We stayed busy running back and forth from the grocery store. I filled the water tanks and checked the fuel. The day before departure, we went up to the marina to check for our package. It was there. It sat in full view of anyone who walked by. The box was bright and conspicuous. Our Fisher CZ21-8 Underwater Metal Detector was on display. A small crowd had gathered around it. They speculated about who it belonged to and what it was for. They were harmless drunks for the most part, but a few of them were capable pirate types. Strong wiry men with dark eyes moved aside as I excused myself. I hoisted the box onto my shoulder and pushed by them towards the exit.

I told Holly to look back and observe who followed us if any did. We made our way towards the dinghy dock. Some of the onlookers had moved to the tiki hut that overlooked the docks. I ignored them, counting on Holly's intuition. We untied the dinghy and left.

"Temple and Rogue," she said. "They were both eyeing us pretty good."

"Rogue?"

"I don't know his real name," she said. "He seems like a nice guy, but he gets into trouble now and then. Drugs maybe."

"And Temple?"

"I've never had a problem with him," she said. "I don't think he's a bad guy, but he's smart enough to know what this thing is for. He's been around the block a few times."

"Anyone else?"

"Just drunks whose boats couldn't move if they wanted to," she said.

"They still watching?"

"Probably," she said. "Hard to tell now."

"We'll go on to the boatyard," I said. "They won't be able to see us down there. Won't know where we went with this."

"An abundance of caution?" she asked.

"Caution, awareness, alertness," I said. "Stay prepared for the worst. Monitor your surroundings. Be ready to act. Stay alive."

"See, this is the kind of talk that gives me pause," she said. "It feels like paranoia."

"Call it what you want," I said. "It's worked for me so far."

"I guess I'm just not as cynical as you are," she said.

"You know how I am," I said. "People suck until they prove otherwise."

"You're probably right," she admitted. "But I just haven't reached that point yet. I just want to waltz through life not worrying about shit. That's why I got the boat, to escape all the drama."

"That's a noble goal," I said. "Meanwhile, I'm being hunted by the FBI. We're on a treasure hunt. We're surrounded by shady characters here. You'd do well to keep your eyes open and your head on a swivel."

"I know it's a dumb question," she said. "But how does this episode end? And what next?"

"We find the gold, or not," I said. "Then we live happily ever after."

"Together?"

"Is that what you want?" I asked.

"Is that what you want?" she asked me. "Never mind. Don't answer that. Just forget it."

"Let's just see this through," I said. "We'll fix Shirl up the best we can. Worry about the rest of it later."

"Typical Breeze," she said.

"I am what I am."

We stashed the detector aboard *Freedom*. The boatyard sits very close to Burdine's, so we went there for a burger. After we ate, we moved to the outside railing to watch the sun go down. It never got old, especially in the Keys. That big orange ball of fire practically sizzled into the sea. The sky lit up with color. We said goodbye to another day. We quietly prayed that the sun would return tomorrow. The sunset was a reliable constant in an otherwise chaotic life.

We didn't spend that night together. We'd endure close quarters togetherness soon enough. We each decided to have one more night in our own heads. She dropped me off at the boatyard and disappeared into the dark.

Freedom was already on the lift. The straps creaked as I climbed aboard. At least I didn't have to endure the tarps and the dust this time. She was all cleaned up and ready to go back in the water. Our prop wash contraption was stowed in the lazarette. I went into the salon. I put a hand on a bulkhead and apologized to *Leap of Faith*.

I'm sorry about the name, old girl. I'll make it right. I promise.

Seven

Holly had an unwanted visit that night from the guy she called Rogue. She came over early to tell me about it. She said that he was clearly tweaking on meth or something similar. He came to steal the metal detector. Holly told him that I had taken it to my boat. When he asked where I was, she told him to go fuck himself. He wanted to know where we were treasure hunting. That's when she pointed a flare gun at him. He backed off, vowing to figure out what we were up to. She had tried to call me on the VHF, but I'd neglected to turn it on. I got scolded for that. She was good about leaving hers on. I wasn't. Other than her, I had no one I wanted to talk to. She wasn't always around, so I kept forgetting to use it when she was.

My boat went back in the water soon after the yard opened for business. They might need the lift for someone else. I tied off to a side pier to wait for nightfall.

"Do you think this dude is going to be trouble?" I asked her. "Or will he sober up and forget about it?"

"He's a strange one," she said. "Sometimes he's completely sane. Occasionally, he goes off the deep end."

"Is it always a drug thing?" I asked. "Or is he bipolar or something?"

"I think it's a bit of both," she said. "Like a lot of folks around here, he needs professional help."

"What could he do to us?" I asked. "He doesn't know where we are."

"He could stalk the marinas," she suggested. "There's not that many to check."

"He doesn't know my boat," I said. "At least not that I know of."

"He could ask around," she countered. "There's always a few drunks at the tiki that are willing to talk."

"My boat was never on a ball this time," I said. "But we were clearly seen and observed at the marina."

"Do you want to leave early?" she asked.

"Maybe we should," I said. "Let's get out of here before he finds us if he hasn't already."

Holly ran back out to her boat to pack a bag and secure things. She made some calls to ask friends to keep an eye on it while she was gone. The regular residents of Boot Key Harbor were good about that sort of thing. There was some occasional petty theft, but it would be tough to trash someone's boat without being seen. Word would go out over the radio. The police would be called. I had the engine running when she got back. I had checked all the thru-hulls in the bilge while she was gone. The old boat had a new look, but she felt the same.

We untied from the pier and idled slowly out of the channel. Howie waved from the parking lot. He'd done another good job for me. He'd also helped to hide me, with few questions asked. He was a gruff old bastard, but he'd come through for me, again. I made a mental note to bring him back something of value. I didn't know if we'd find any gold chains, but I owed him something.

"Do you want to just head straight for the bridge?" asked Holly. "Or do you want to throw them off our trail?"

"How so?" I asked. "I'm open to suggestions."

"Go Oceanside," she said. "We'll go up to the Channel Five bridge and use the old yacht channel to Cape Sable."

"Good idea," I said. "Unless someone actually follows us in a boat, they'll think we went up the Keys."

"It's not even that far out of the way," she said. "Couple extra hours maybe."

We headed east out of Marathon towards Islamorada. The seas ran with us. Two-foot waves gently rolled under our hull. Puffy white clouds contrasted with the sapphire blue sky. We took a course close to the reef to avoid lobster traps until we neared the Channel Five Bridge.

"Sailboat behind us," Holly called out. "Six o'clock and holding steady."

"How long's he been back there?" I asked.

"I don't know," she said. "Just noticed him."

"Where'd he come from?"

"Must have come out of Sister's Creek," she said.

"So it's from Boot Key," I said. "Great."

"We don't know that it's following us," she said. "Give me the binoculars."

Holly went aft and studied the boat behind us for a long time. She asked me to slow down. She wanted it to get closer. She wanted a better look. I eased back on the throttle and the mystery boat slowly gained on us.

"I'm not going to swear to it," said Holly. "But it looks like Rabble's boat."

"You've got to be shitting me," I said. "No way."

"Do you want to let him get closer to find out?" she asked. "Or speed up and pull away?"

"Whenever you sense trouble, leave it behind you," I said. "Let's roll."

"Aye aye, captain," she said. "Full steam ahead."

I brought the throttle back forward until we hit eight knots. We went under the bridge and picked up the yacht channel near the ICW.

We were pulling away from our shadow boat easily. If it was Rabble, seeing him was no coincidence. I didn't put much stock in coincidence. I kept hammering north. The boat behind us got smaller and smaller. We'd lose it long before we neared our hunting grounds. Still, the thought of Rabble trailing us was unsettling. He had a score to settle with me.

We kept chugging north and up the west coast of Florida. Holly took over somewhere off the Ten Thousand Islands. I ate a sandwich and took a nap. The wind had fallen off to nothing. It was great trawler weather, but not so good for a sailboat. We were putting a lot of miles between us and our pursuer if we even had a pursuer. It was a familiar situation for me. I'd run away from phantom followers a bunch of times. Some of them were real. So far, I'd managed to stay ahead of all of them.

When I was by myself, I'd stop several times along the coast. It would take me three or four days to make the trip from the Keys to Pelican Bay. Having another capable captain on board meant that we could keep traveling through the night. The only problem was, that we were both a bit tired by the time we arrived at Cayo Costa. We dropped anchor outside the bay over our target area. We just didn't have enough gumption to get started on our search. We decided to rest for a few hours before setting up our first dive.

The nap lasted longer than expected. I woke up four hours later. It was late afternoon. We still had plenty of daylight left, but not really enough time to mount a serious effort. Holly was playing with the metal detector when I came up out of my bunk.

"If it ain't Rip Van Winkle," she said. "I thought you might sleep all night."

"I guess I'm not getting any younger," I said. "Why didn't you wake me up?"

"You must have needed the sleep," she said. "And I need you sharp when I go down there."

"How do you want to go at this?" I asked.

"I use the detector first," she answered. "Then we use the prop wash to clear any area that I get a hit on."

"We'll need some buoys to mark the spots," I suggested. "I've got some fishing sinkers. We can use water bottles as floats."

"I've been reading the manual for this thing," she said. "I can rule out small pings as bottle caps or whatever. The big pings get a marker. How do we get the boat in the right spot?"

"Stern anchors," I said. "We drop the main anchor out front and use the current to drop back over the target. Then we deploy two stern anchors off each corner. That should hold us when we put the motor in gear."

"Will I be able to swivel the barrel?" she asked.

"Only up and down," I replied. "It won't articulate from side to side."

"What if we miss the target?"

"We use the anchors to reposition the boat," I said.

"Tedious work," she said.

"If it's only a small adjustment, we can just put some slack in one and tighten up the other," I said. "If not, we'll have to physically lift and relocate the anchors until we're where we want to be."

"I don't think I can carry them underwater," she said. "You'll have to do it."

"I can do it if it comes to that," I said. "We'll just have to play around with it. See how it works."

"Rig me up some buoys," she said. "I'll make a few exploratory runs with the detector. I want to get a feel for how it works."

I dug around in my old tackle bags until I found the heavier weights. I had plenty of monofilament to use as a line. I chugged a Gatorade and tied the empty bottle to the line. I tossed a bottle of water to Holly and told her to drink it.

"Make sure you keep hydrated out here," I reminded her.

"I see how you hydrate," she said. "I don't think beer qualifies as hydration."

"Beer is the nectar of the Gods," I told her. "Don't want to disturb them."

"I'm going to go disturb the fishes," she said. "Put the dive flag up and keep an eye out."

She hopped off the swim platform and sank below the surface. She popped right back up, adjusted her mask and grabbed the detector. It had earphones to transmit beeps when it detected metal. The water quality was even worse than before, so visibility would be at a minimum. She'd been down about five minutes when I saw the sailboat coming into the Boca Grande Pass. I tugged at her air hose, signaling her to the surface.

She stuck her head up behind the boat and gave me a quizzical look. I pointed out to the Pass.

"You think it's the same boat?" she asked.

"Can't tell yet," I said. "But you should come back aboard, just in case."

I went for the binoculars while she climbed on the boat. I stood up on the bow for an unobstructed view. It looked like the same boat from the previous day. Holly came to my side. I handed her the binoculars. She focused and stared at the oncoming vessel for a long time.

"It's him," she said. "It's fucking Rabble. He's got someone else with him. Another dude."

"Unbelievable."

"How do you think they found us," she asked.

"I don't know," I admitted. "Maybe someone in the boatyard talked. Gave us up. Maybe that Rogue fellow found us there. Told Rabble what to look for."

"Then it's probably Rogue on the boat with him," she said. "I don't like this."

"I don't much like it either," I said. "I'm grabbing the shotgun."

I went below and unwrapped the twenty gauge from its oiled cloth. I worked the slide a couple of times, then loaded it with buckshot. Back on the bow, Holly was using the binoculars again.

"They're coming right at us," she said.

I watched them as they lowered the sails and slowed down. By the time they got close to us, their boat was barely moving. The engine was running. They maneuvered to within thirty feet, stopping and hovering alongside.

"Fancy meeting you here," said Rabble.

"What do you want?" I asked, making sure he could see my weapon.

"We want a piece of whatever action you have going on here," he said. "We know about the detector. We know about the prop wash rig you had built."

"Why would I let you anywhere near us?" I asked. "Beat it, or eat some buckshot."

"It's like this," Rabble said. "My friend Rogue here didn't hear the Coast Guard broadcasts looking for your ass, but I did. The two of us put our knowledge together. Call it blackmail if you want. They're looking for *Leap of Faith*. I know what your boat is named now, and what it looks like now. I don't know why they want you, but it doesn't matter. I'll just make a phone call and the cops will be here shortly."

"Shit," said Holly. "You should have fed him to the gators when you had the chance."

That sparked an idea in my brain. I had let him live. I could have easily wasted him and left him up Little Shark River. He wouldn't have been found for a very long time. No one would have ever known it was me. He'd have been just another body in the Glades. It happens more than you think.

"I could have killed you easily," I said. "But I didn't."

"Your mistake, I guess," he said. "What's that got to do with anything?"

"I also let you keep some of the money you stole," I reminded him. "I gave you a fighting chance."

"That you did," he admitted. "I didn't really understand why."

"I'm not the bad guy here," I said. "You were the thief. I was simply recovering what was taken from my friend."

"That's beside the point," he said. "Either you cut us in, or I call cops."

"I won't let you work with us," I told him. "You can't be trusted. You don't deserve it either, but there's a way I can cut you in."

"Keep talking," he said.

"Hold on," I said, handing the gun to Holly. "I'll be right back."

I went back inside and grabbed one of the gold bars. I came out and showed it to Rabble. His eyes got big. I gave it to Holly and took back the gun. She posed with the shiny gold like a model on The Price is Right. I was taking a chance, gambling that Rabble would keep his word.

"When I found you," I said. "I took ten grand in cash. This bar is worth ten grand."

"How many of them do you have?" he asked.

"We only found two," I told him. "I'm offering you half of everything we've recovered so far."

"In exchange for what, exactly?" he asked.

"If you accept," I said. "Then you and I are good. Even up. Understand?"

"I keep my mouth shut," he said. "I take the gold and leave you alone."

"It's either that or I blow your head off," I said. "Your choice."

"How do you know I won't take the gold, then turn you in later?"

"I let you live once," I said. "It won't happen again."

I saw movement out of the corner of my eye. Rogue was pointing a pistol out of a port light. Boom! Buckshot splattered the glass and punched a dozen holes in the surrounding fiberglass. I racked the slide and aimed back at Rabble. He raised his hands up.

"Man, I had nothing to do with that," he said. "The dude ain't right in the head."

The shotgun blast had taken away his cockiness.

"Take him away from here, Rabble," I said. "Go on back to the Keys. Leave us alone."

"The gold?" he asked.

"Stand by," I said.

I had Holly put the gold bar in the dinghy. We had a long line attaching it to the boat. She let it drop back behind us a good fifty feet. I kept the shotgun trained on Rabble. Rogue remained below. I didn't want to allow them to get close enough to us to cause damage.

"I've got stern anchors coming off each corner back there," I told Rabble. "Swing wide and come up between them. Take the gold and leave immediately."

"Considering the circumstances, this is a fair deal," he said. "I'll keep quiet. You have my word."

"You're ten thousand dollars richer, and you're still alive," I said. "Pretty good day if you ask me."

"Truce, brother," he said. "I'll steer clear of you from now on."

"Best idea you've had lately," I said. "Go back out the Pass so we can watch you."

Rogue came up to steer the boat. He had a bloody rag around one hand. As soon as he pulled up to the dinghy, Rabble jumped down to retrieve the gold. He scrambled back onto his boat within seconds. He was quick and nimble.

"Go out the Pass, now," I yelled.

He nodded his agreement, nudged Rogue away from the helm, and motored away. I didn't relax my grip on the shotgun until they were out of sight.

"There goes ten grand," said Holly. "You think he'll hold up his end of the bargain?"

"One can hope," I said. "Don't worry about the gold. We still have three of them. Tomorrow we'll find a bunch more."

"I'm just remembering how you told me this little expedition wouldn't be dangerous," she said.

"We just had a little unplanned inconvenience," I said. "I handled it."

"That gunshot scared the shit out of me," she said.

"Nothing to be afraid of now," I said. "Except sharks."

I pointed at a dorsal fin slicing the surface. We both watched a ten-foot hammerhead swim through our search area.

Eight

We took turns on watch that night. I wanted to make sure that Rabble didn't return in the dark. He did not. Holly was on deck during the early morning hours when the wind picked up. It started blowing out of the northwest, making things uncomfortable. The motion woke me. Before I could finish my first cup of coffee, it increased to twenty-five knots and made things miserable for us both.

We grudgingly pulled up anchor and retreated to the shelter of Pelican Bay.

"This little expedition is off to a flying start," Holly said. "I think we may be jinxed."

"Temporary setback," I said. "It will give us some time to refine our plan."

"How so?" she asked.

"The current is a problem," I began. "We need to set up some sort of search grid, so we don't keep going over the same area."

"I can't see shit down near the bottom," she said. "I'm flying blind."

"How can we lay lines on the bottom?" I asked. "If we could anchor down a square, you could pull yourself along a straight line."

"I've got to hold the detector at the same time," she said. "I've only got two hands."

"So we make it visible somehow," I said. "Any ideas?"

"Aluminum foil?" she asked.

"We could strap a dive light on your head," I suggested.

"It's pretty redneck," she said. "But it might work. Search a square, then flip it over to form a new square."

"I've got a bunch of old lines in the lazarette," I said. "Dig them out. I'll look for something to use as weights."

I had one big spare anchor and a dinghy anchor. I needed at least two more heavy objects. I dug around in the forward berth but came up empty. I looked around in the bilge compartments, finding nothing suitable. I emptied out the storage spaces on the bridge. I found nothing. I asked Holly to poke around where she was. She found nothing there that would work. It was a simple enough thing. I just needed something heavy to hold a line down under water. A big rock would do it. That's it, I thought. I'd seen milk crates in the bilge. I used them to hold extra oil and coolant. I could fill them with rocks. They'd be easy to tie lines to.

"Now you're going off the charts redneck," Holly said.

"Just a little southern ingenuity," I said. "You make do with what's available."

"Can we incorporate some bailing twine and duct tape?" she asked. "We need to cover all the redneck bases."

"Funny," I said. "How much line did you come up with?"

"I can make a forty foot square," she reported.

"Great. Now let's go find some rocks."

Who knew how hard it was to find rocks on Cayo Costa? There weren't any. Not even a pebble. All we could think of to do was fill the milk crates with shells. We collected the bigger clam shells, and a few horse conchs until we had two crates full. They weighed about ten pounds each. It would have to do. We carted our makeshift anchors back to the boat and spent the afternoon rigging up lines. The wind stayed steady at twenty-five all day. We studied the marks we'd made on the handheld GPS, and transferred them to the boat's main unit.

It gave us an idea where Holly had already searched, but we didn't have the detector the first time. We decided to start on fresh territory, just beyond where we'd looked before. I grabbed a beer for happy hour. Holly mixed up a concoction of mango nectar, cranberry juice, and Sprite. It looked like a tequila sunrise. I held up my beer can to her glass.

"Cheers to redneck ingenuity," I said.

"Cheers to finding gold," she replied.

We sat and drank until the sun went down. In spite of the setbacks, and our primitive equipment, we both felt optimistic.

We opted not to stand watch that night. Instead, I slept up in the salon, with my shotgun close at hand. We had no unwanted visitors. I assumed that Rabble and Rogue had left the area for good. I dreamt of a mountain of gold bars, a bathtub full of gold coins, and an army of little golden idols.

I awoke to calmer winds and the smell of bacon cooking. Holly was in the galley wearing one of my shirts and nothing else. Her hair was a wreck, but when she smiled at me I thought she was as pretty as any model. I tried to grab her ass but she fended me off with a spatula.

"Pancakes coming up," she said.

"You're awesome," I said. "Thanks."

"I needed something to do while you got your beauty sleep," she said, laughing.

"Did you check the weather?" I asked.

"South at ten knots," she answered. "Slight chance of afternoon thunderstorms."

"It will be nice and calm out there," I said. "You ready to find some gold?"

"Raring to go," she said. "Get a good breakfast and go kick some ass."

After we ate, I pulled out all the parts for our prop wash rig. Holly arranged our search grid lines. We raised the anchor and crawled through the bay and out around the point to our target zone. I positioned the boat over our desired location and dropped the anchor. We looked around for other boats. No one was in sight. We looked up at the sky. It was clear and sunny.

"Let's roll," I said.

"Try to keep up, old man," she replied.

We both went underwater to arrange the search grid. The sun hit the foil at times, making it visible, but it really lit up when Holly's dive light shined on it. We formed a square on the bottom with our anchors and crates full of shells. She gave me the thumbs up and we returned to the surface. She sat on the swim platform while I went up to the bridge to take another look around. I saw no boats. I saw no shark fins either.

"Now or never," I said. "Looks all clear."

"Let's do this," she answered.

I handed her the underwater metal detector. She clipped a weight and buoy to her dive belt. Down she went. I stayed up to maintain a watch. It only took ten minutes for her to sweep the square. She popped her head up behind the boat.

"I got a hit just outside the square," she said. "Decent signal. I tried to dig it up but it's too deep."

"You want to try the prop wash?" I asked.

"We're going to have to rig it up sooner or later," she said.

"Put your buoy on it," I said. "I need the anchors to position the boat."

"I'll lose my square," she said.

"Bring it up here," I said. "We'll put some snap swivels on the ends of the line. Pop it off and on real quick."

"Why didn't you think of that before we put it down there?" she asked.

"Why didn't you?" I asked back. "I can't think of everything."

"You can't?" she said, laughing. "I thought you always had everything covered."

"I try," I said.

We re-tied the lines with snap swivels. I put longer lines on the anchors and drug them out behind the boat. We tugged and pulled on them until the boat swung over the buoy. I had to let out a little more chain on the main anchor to back up some. We both got under the swim platform and assembled the brackets and barrel. It was a clunky process. Turning wrenches under water wasn't a simple task. A dropped nut was a lost nut. We struggled with it but finally won the battle. We expended too much energy in the process, so a break was required. We drank some water and caught our breath.

"How's this going to work?" asked Holly.

"I start the engine and put it in gear," I explained. "The anchors will hold us in place. The prop will produce a force that is redirected down towards the bottom. You can swivel the barrel slightly, up or down. The sand below will be washed away, revealing the object. At least, that's the idea."

"I'm ready when you are," she said.

I fired up the engine. Holly went under. I put it in forward and gave it a little throttle. The anchor lines off the stern pulled tight. The water behind the boat swirled downward. I couldn't see Holly down below the bottom of the boat until she stuck her head up. She stuck a closed fist up in the air and yelled for me to stop. I throttled down and pulled it out of gear.

"Jesus," she said. "We blew sand everywhere. I can't see a thing now."

"It'll settle down," I said. "Or the current will carry it away."

It took ten minutes for the sediment to clear out. Holly went back down with the detector. She came back up with a rusted hunk of metal. It was cylindrical in shape and badly corroded. It might have been a starter solenoid at one time. It certainly wasn't a gold bar. We'd spent hours to find someone's discarded motor part. Holly wasn't deterred. She was young and fit and ready to try again.

She rearranged the grid and started another sweep. She got another ping from the detector. I went down and moved the anchors to reposition the boat once again. The engine was started and the prop wash blew at the bottom another time. Holly came up with the fist again. I stopped the wash.

"You blew the baskets of shells over and they went flying," she said. "The buoy moved too."

"Can you look again with the detector?" I asked.

"I'll have to let the shit storm settle again."

"This isn't going so well, is it?"

"We need better gear," she said. "Maybe stakes in the bottom instead of anchors and shells."

Eventually, she could see well enough to go back and relocate the object that pinged the detector. It was a small Danforth anchor with about three feet of chain attached. Some fisherman had lost it here a long time ago. The chain was encrusted in barnacles. It wasn't gold, but we could use it to anchor the grid lines. I considered it a small victory. Maybe it was a good sign.

Unfortunately, the day was growing old. Time flies when you're hunting treasure. We still had to disassemble the prop wash rig if we wanted to move the boat. Holly wanted to leave it on and just stay anchored outside the bay. I saw her point, but I was worried that something would come up. If we needed to move, it would be difficult with the prop wash aimed at the bottom. In an emergency, we'd need the ability to start up and go in an instant. We worked together to remove the barrel, leaving the brackets and supports in place.

We'd worked hard. We'd fumbled with our poor excuse for equipment. We'd only managed to search two squares. We needed to regroup. It would take weeks at that slow pace unless we got extremely lucky. The back deck was a tangle of aluminum foil covered ropes, anchors, and a blue barrel. We were short one corner of our square. It was not a good day.

"Let's go treasure hunting," Holly said. "It'll be fun, they said."

"I guess we don't really know what we're doing," I said. "This is hard work."

"We just aren't prepared," she said. "We need a hardware store."

"I don't think I should be hanging out in public around here," I said. "No sense in making myself easy to find."

"Oh yeah," she said. "I almost forgot about the whole FBI thing."

"We need a different approach," I said. "This is too clumsy. Let me drink on it for a while."

"Think on it?" she asked.

"Think, drink, same thing," I answered. "Helps to lubricate my brain."

I started drinking on it with a few cold beers. When that failed to produce, I added some octane in the form of rum. The problem was a combination of limited resources, limited knowledge, and adverse conditions. For all we knew, we were chasing the half-baked dreams of a slightly senile old sailor. We didn't know if there was gold to be found. We didn't know how to find it if it was actually down there. We were totally winging it, as I was prone to do. I had tried to be methodical and approach the search logically and mathematically. That was against my instincts. I decided to change our strategy. To hell with logic. We could just swim around with the detector, blow some sand around and see what happens.

"Take apart the square," I told Holly. "Tag a ping with the small weight and buoy first. Then we come back with an anchor and a bigger buoy. We can use fenders. We'll drive over the buoy and expose the object. We've got three anchors and plenty of fenders. Find three objects. We'll sweep all of them in one pass."

"That will be faster," she said. "But I'll just be swimming around willy-nilly."

"We'll give it a shot," I said. "You can swim the whole area in a few days this way. If we don't hit anything good, screw it. We'll pack up and leave."

"I'll keep trying until we run out of food and water," she said.

"That's my girl."

Nine

The air hose on the hookah rig was only fifty feet long. It was too much trouble to keep moving the big boat, so we transferred the rig into the dinghy. I could follow her around as needed, allowing her more time underwater. We went back to marker seventy-five and took new bearings, basically starting the search from square one. We knew where Holly had found the last two bars. We assumed that if there were more, they would be nearby. I had rigged up several more small buoys for Holly to mark likely spots with.

She made her first dive of the day just after breakfast. I watched as first one, then two, then three buoys popped up to the surface. They were roughly fifty feet apart, almost in a straight line. I went over the side with the fenders attached to heavy anchors. I secured the anchors deep in the sand and let the fenders float above me. We were ready to make a pass with the prop wash rig.

Again, we struggled to mount the barrel that would direct the water downward. It was an ungainly contraption. It took forever to get it attached just right. The effort wore me out. Holly was much better at that sort of work then I was. She was still fresh. She stayed in the water to observe. I started the engine, pulled anchor, and slowly positioned the boat for a run at the markers we'd planted. I motored over them at three knots, looking back to see the sand swirling in my wake.

Once I had completed the course, I idled alongside Holly.

"You went over them too fast," she said. "We didn't displace much sand. Just made a mess."

"Did the anchors hold?" I asked.

"They didn't move," she said. "We need to slow you down without diminishing the force we're using towards the bottom."

"An anchor would work," I said. "But I'm fresh out."

"Can we use your bow anchor?" she asked.

"I suppose so," I replied. "Give me five minutes."

I went to the bow and removed the forty-four pound Bruce anchor from the pulpit. I didn't have any extra chain to attach to it, but I didn't need it to actually hold the boat in place. I just needed something to create enough drag to slow the boat without reducing rpms. I tied two long dock lines together and attached them to the anchor. I dropped it off the stern and played out the lines.

"This anchor is going to create its own sandstorm as I drag it along," I told Holly.

"The prop wash should take care of it," she said. "It's right under and behind the prop."

"Okay, here's goes nothing," I said.

I eased the throttle forward for another run at the fenders. The anchor tried to stop me, but eventually, it drug along the bottom. I was barely moving, so I increased throttle. I looked back to see a whirlwind of sand, shells, and sediment blowing out behind me. It was working. Then Holly popped up, waving both arms in the air. I pulled back on the throttle and took the boat out of gear. She swam towards me. I shut the engine off.

"It's tearing up the barrel," she said. "The bolts are pulling right through it."

"That stern anchor will hold us still for now," I said. "Let's wait for the dust to settle. See what we've done down there."

We sat on the swim platform and shared a bottle of water. The current was strong enough to carry away most of the debris in short order. The incoming tide was clean. Clarity increased as we watched.

"Are you excited?" I asked Holly. "You might have some gold waiting for you down there."

"Or a crab trap, a tire rim, and somebody's old washing machine," she said.

"Go take a look," I said. "I'll check on the barrel."

She used the dinghy to position herself over the first fender. I dove under the swim platform to check on the damage to our prop wash rig. Holly was right. The bolts were pulling through the plastic. Each side now had a foot-long tunnel as the bolts wore their way down. I could take the bolts out, spin the barrel a bit, then make new holes and remount it. That would take some time and effort. I climbed back aboard to grab some wrenches. I had my back to the transom when Holly surfaced I heard her whoop.

I spun around to see her holding one gold bar over her head. She wore the biggest smile I'd ever seen on a human being. She did a little water dance, spinning in a circle and waving the bar around. Whoop whoop! I applauded her from the back deck. She plopped the bar in the dinghy, climbed into it herself, and made her way back to me.

"Hot damn, Breeze," she exclaimed. "There's gold in them there waters."

"Shirley wasn't so crazy after all," I said.

"I'm pumped now," she said. "Let me take the detector back down there while you fix the barrel."

"I need you to help me with it," I said. "I can't hold it up and put bolts through it at the same time."

"Crap," she said. "I want to get back down there."

"How deep did we dig with the prop wash?" I asked.

"It's a good trench," she said. "About three foot deep and four feet wide. This bar was laying in the bottom of the trench. There's got to be more."

"That's too deep for us to dig by hand," I said. "We need to fix the barrel."

"I'll help you get it aboard," she said. "Then I'll go down with the detector while you drill new holes."

"Then I go down to move the big anchors and fenders," I said. "You're going to wear me out."

"I told you to try to keep up," she said, laughing. "Come on old man. Let's get some gold."

We both worked to remove the damaged barrel. I knew that we'd have the same problem again. We'd only get so many more passes before the barrel was useless. I kept that to myself, though. We dragged it on board. Before I could get a drill, Holly was back in the water with the detector. I moved slowly, trying to catch my breath and rest a little bit. By the time I finished drilling new holes, I saw the first small buoy pop up. A few minutes later, a second buoy appeared.

Then a third almost instantly. They made a triangle with ten-foot sides. Holly's head appeared. She smiled up at me.

"I think we've found it," she said. "The detector pings all over the place between those floats. It's like one big piece of metal."

"Take a break," I told her. "I'll move one anchor into the center of it."

I was tired, but the possibility of hitting the motherlode pumped me up. I'd do the heavy lifting, but I'd let Holly be the one to discover what we'd found. I hoped it wasn't a sunken steel hull. I hoped it was Shirley's gold. We still had to reattach the barrel before we could blast away the target area. I'd be out of gas after that.

Once the prop wash rig was reassembled, we repeated the process. The big stern anchor kept the boat slowed down. The prop wash ate away at the bottom, throwing sand and debris. I slowly dug another trench through the triangle. Holly hung off the side of the dinghy, waiting for the water to clear. She was still smiling like a monkey with a new banana. She couldn't contain herself for long. She descended while the water was still roiled up.

I pulled the stern anchor until it was off of the bottom. I went back to the helm and positioned the big boat next to the dinghy. Just as I grabbed a line to bring the little boat in, I saw it.

Our hammerhead had returned. I quickly tied off the dinghy, jumped into it and yanked hard on Holly's air hose. I knew she wouldn't want to surface so quickly, so I gave it a double yank. She came up slowly. I wanted her to hurry. When her hand cleared the surface, I grabbed it and started pulling her aboard. She sensed something was wrong, and quickly scrambled in.

"What is it?" she asked.

"Shark's back," I said.

"Fuck," she said. "There's a shitload of gold down there."

"For real?" I asked.

"For real, Breeze," she replied. "Fifty bars or more, plus some other stuff."

"Coins, jewelry?"

"Little men," she said. "Idols, gods, whatever. It was still too cloudy to make out detail."

"Holy shit," I said. "Son of a bitch."

"We're going to be rich."

We sat and watched the big shark patrol the area. He swam along the edges of the clouds we'd made with the prop wash, investigating. He stayed with the cloud as the current carried it away. We were drifting too, I realized. I quickly redeployed the stern anchor to stop us. The floating fender was still in place. We knew where the gold was. I doubted that the shark gave a shit about gold.

"Start the engine," I told Holly. "I'll put this anchor back on the bow. We'll position our aft end over that fender."

"What about the shark?" she asked.

"Wait him out," I said. "He's just curious. He'll leave to find something to eat sooner or later."

"He was here the other day," she said. "This must be his turf."

"Assuming it's the same one," I said. "Lots of hammerheads in these waters."

We got the main anchor reattached, circled around and situated the boat so that it would back down on the fender. At first, I backed right over it, but I pulled in anchor chain until it popped up under the swim platform. We were sitting on a pile of gold. We didn't see the shark any longer, but neither of us was in a hurry to jump overboard.

"What did you see down there?" I asked.

"Neatly lined rows of gold bars," she said. "Like a tile floor."

"What about the figurines?"

Every tenth space or so, was a little statue, instead of a bar," she said. "I could only pick them up with the flashlight. Should be cleared up by now."

"We've still got that shark to worry about," I said. "When we're ready, even if we don't spot him, we should work quickly. Nobody stays down for more than a minute or two."

"We need a basket to load them in," she said.

"My silly milk crates should work," I said. "Lousy anchors. Good baskets."

"I'll tie a harness on one," she said. "Lines to each corner. One line to the boat."

"Sailors and their knots," I said. "Finally found a good use for them."

She punched my arm hard.

"Stink potter," she said.

"Rag hauler," I replied.

"Oil burner."

"Blow boater."

"We do have one thing in common," she said.

"I can think of a few," I said.

"I'm talking about a healthy respect for sharks," she said.

"I call it fear," I replied. "I want nothing to do with that thing."

"Gold won't do me much good if I'm bitten in half," she said.

"True story," I said. "Let's just wait until one of us can't stand it anymore."

"I'll get brave, sooner or later," she said. "But not right now."

So we settled in to wait him out. We watched the water. Happy hour rolled around so I popped a beer. Dinner time arrived. We watched the water. We ate grilled cheese sandwiches and chips. The sun got lower. We watched the water. The sun set over the Gulf of Mexico. We never saw the shark again that night, but neither of us got brave enough to dive. We transferred our nervous energy to the bedroom. We hadn't discussed the meaning of our relationship since the gold expedition began. We'd been preoccupied with the mission. We'd been working well together. That night, we worked together in a different way. It was good for both of us.

Ten

The storm hit sometime after midnight. A loud crack of thunder woke us both. I'd been too distracted to check the weather or the radar. First, it was the gold. Then it was the sex. I'd lost awareness of my situation, and put my boat at risk. The storm itself shouldn't have been any big deal, but we were totally exposed to it. Our little pile of treasure wasn't in any sort of reasonable anchorage, it was in open water, very near the Gulf. The Boca Grande Pass ran deep and strong just a few hundred yards away. It wasn't a good place to ride out a storm.

We should have made careful marks on the GPS, anchored inside the bay for the night, and kept safety as our first concern. We had failed to do that. Now the storm was upon us. I didn't want to leave the fender floating. It would be an obvious indication that something was below it. Any fool that came along would investigate.

"What do you want to do?" asked Holly. "The boat is rocking pretty good out here."

"If we run for cover, we need to pull up the fender," I said. "We can't leave it out here unattended."

"The barrel is still in place," she reminded me.

"Shit," I said. "We can't make way in these waves with it in place."

"We can't get it off either," she said. "We'd get clobbered under there."

"I guess we're riding it out then," I said. "Poor decision making on my part."

"It's my fault too," she admitted. "Gold, sharks, sunset, and sex. I took my eye off the ball too."

"A lesson for us both," I said. "It's going to be a long night."

"At least if we drag," she started. "We won't hit anything for miles."

"Make a waypoint right here," I said. "In case we do drag."

"Should we put out some more chain?"

"Can't," I said. "We don't want to risk wrapping that fender line up in the prop."

"Sitting ducks," she said.

"Been through worse," I said. "Morgan's Bluff comes to mind."

She shrugged. I shrugged. We brought blankets and pillows up into the salon and tried to make ourselves comfortable. It didn't work, but it felt good to have someone close during the storm. Lightning streaked across the sky out over the Gulf. Thunder rumbled deep in my bones. The old boat creaked and groaned as the waves tossed her up and down. Eventually, exhaustion took over and I fell asleep. I had no idea that we were slowly dragging the anchor.

When we woke up in the morning, the boat had moved almost a thousand yards. We were on a shallow grass flat just outside the entrance to Pelican Bay. The hull was resting gently on the sand. We weren't hard aground, just touching bottom. The tide was coming in, so we'd float off in an hour or two. Holly went down to check on the prop and rudder just in case we'd done damage. She came back up with a fender in her hand.

"Our marker got caught up in the prop when we dragged," she said. "The blue barrel is gone."

"We've got a good GPS mark on our spot," I said. "Won't be hard to find it again."

"The prop and rudder are okay," she reported. "The keel is just barely touching bottom."

"Some good news, at least," I said. "I'll use the windlass to pull us further out."

Holly stayed in the water while I cranked the windlass. Anchor chain came aboard and was routed into the chain locker. The boat inched forward. I bumped it a few feet at a time, not wanting to ruin the windlass. Pulling up the chain by hand got old real fast. Eventually, Holly signaled that we were floating free of the bottom. The incoming tide would put another two feet of water under our keel. We ate some breakfast before starting the engine and returning to the search area. The storm had long passed. We had a gentle sea and a cloud-proof sky.

Holly took care of some maintenance on the hookah rig while I disassembled what was left of our prop wash rig. When she was ready, we switched places. She went under with the metal detector and a new marker. Ten minutes later she came up, shaking her head.

"I found it," she said. "But it's covered up with sand again."

"How deep?" I asked.

"Maybe a foot," she answered. "You can just make out where the trench was. I dug around a little with my hands but didn't find anything. Couldn't get deep enough."

"That's going to make things difficult," I said. "We can't blow the sand away without the barrel."

"I don't suppose you keep a shovel on board, do you?" she asked.

"As a matter of fact, I do," I told her. "It's a fold-up job that I bought at an Army/Navy store."

"I won't even ask why you bought a shovel," she said.

"I used it to plant dope," I said. "I had a couple dozen plants all over this island. Might still be some out there, growing wild."

"You don't say," she said. "You know, I quit drinking, but I wouldn't mind getting high."

"Knock yourself out," I said. "We can go look after we get finished here."

"Cool beans," she said. "I'm going to need a weight belt if I want to dig with a shovel under water."

She dug around in her dive bag until she found it. I dusted off the folding shovel. We put one of her waist weights in the milk crate to help sink it to the bottom. There was no sign of sharks.

"Remember," I said. "A couple of minutes and you come up. Don't play around down there. I'll keep an eye out for that old hammerhead."

"You see a shark," she said. "Yank that air hose right out of my mouth."

"I'll let you know."

I watched her slowly descend. The incoming tide had given us cleaner water, in spite of the storm. I could just make out the dive light strapped to her head. Her digging clouded things down there. She tugged on the line that was tied to the milk crate. I brought it up. Four gold bars came up with it. Holly came up close behind.

"I cleared off some of it," she said. "Lots more where that came from."

"Come aboard," I told her. "Shark watch."

We both scanned the surface. No dorsal fins were spotted. I went up to the bridge to get a better downward angle. I didn't see anything. I nodded to Holly. She slid back under, dragging the milk crate with her. I stayed on the bridge, keeping watch. I didn't notice when Holly yanked on the milk crate rope. She stuck her head up and hollered.

"Pull me up," she said. "I got you a present."

I quickly scrambled down to the lower deck. She climbed aboard while I brought up the crate. It contained four more bars and one little gold man. I lifted the strange figure out of the crate. He had a big round belly and chest. His arms curved out from his body like the handle of a coffee cup. They reattached at his waist. He had a bulbous nose with wide nostrils. He wore an elaborate headdress with spikes protruding from the top. Big hoop earrings dangled from his lobes. The detail was astonishing. You could see his carved teeth and the necklace he wore. He even sported a tiny penis. He didn't look like a friendly guy. He looked angry. A small dick will do that to some guys. I didn't know if it was Aztec, or Incan, or something from a novelty store, but it felt heavy like gold. It was clearly the same metal that the bars were formed from. I was convinced we had a genuine ancient artifact on our hands. It was the key to turning simple gold bars into an internationally sought after treasure.

"Well?" said Holly.

"I think it's the real deal," I said. "Might be worth millions."

"Wahoo!" she screamed.

She tried to do a little dance on the deck, but her clumsy dive flippers tripped her up. I caught her on the way down. We both toppled over. I held tight to the little gold man. I held tight to Holly. We kissed briefly, then began laughing our asses off.

"I can't believe it," she said. "Your stupid blue barrel. Your silly milk crates full of shells. There is no way we should be sitting on a fortune in gold."

"You did all the hard work," I said. "The credit goes to you, not my lame jury-rigging."

"Let's not forget Shirley," she reminded me. "We both doubted her."

"That salty old coot," I said. "She's found her gold at last."

We laughed some more. The absurdity of the situation was not lost on us. We were giddy with gold fever. Then the hammerhead reappeared. Our laughing stopped.

"Go away, you son of a bitch," I yelled. "We've got work to do here."

"That thing gives me the willies," said Holly. "Can't we shoot him?"

"That would bring attention to us real fast," I said. "The rangers would call the cops or the Coast Guard."

"Nothing happened when you blasted Rabble's boat," she said.

"True, but that was a one-shot deal," I said. "What's it take to kill a big hammerhead?"

"Blood in the water will attract his buddies," she added.

"Send up the bat signal," I said. "Ask for some shark repellent."

"I can't go down there now," she said. "Gold or no gold."

"We'll wait him out," I said. "Again."

The shark was a menacing figure, gliding around my boat. There's something primordial about watching a killing machine up close and personal. Neither of us doubted that he would attack if we got in the water. He was taunting us. He was making it clear that this was his turf. He was the top of the food chain here, not man. Our thirst for gold was put on hold as long as he remained in the area. He decided to remain all afternoon.

"How big you figure he is?" Holly asked.

"I'd guess ten feet," I answered. "But fish always look bigger in the water."

"Big enough," she said.

"There used to be a bigger one out in the Pass," I said. "Showed up every tarpon season. The locals called him *Old Hitler*. He wasn't afraid of boats or people. He'd just swim around, waiting for someone to hook a tarpon. Then he'd steal it."

"Not very sporting," she said. "Why didn't people just stop fishing when he was around?"

"The good guides would," I said. "They understood that a weak and tired tarpon couldn't get away from *Old Hitler*, but the weekenders would keep right on fishing. I think they liked to see the blood and gore it caused."

"Let's not think about blood and gore," she said. "What are we going to do about him?"

"It's getting late," I said. "Let's try again tomorrow."

"I really hate to leave this spot," she said. "We're so close."

"I don't want a replay of last night," I said. "Check the radar. Let's get secured. The gold isn't going anywhere."

Storms were brewing over the Gulf. We raised anchor and sought the safety of Pelican Bay. I had enough time to finish my first beer before we got hit. Summer storms in Florida are no joke. Most people don't realize how violent they can be. They sit in the air-conditioning and barely realize it's raining. On a boat, you've got a front row seat to strong gusty winds, sideways rain, and dangerous lightning. We were safe. The anchor was well set. We had some protection from the wind. It could get choppy in the bay, but you never saw the big waves that rolled outside.

It lasted an hour. The sun returned just in time to set. We ate a light dinner. The mosquitoes prevented us from sitting on the deck, so we shared a seat on the settee.

"What will you do with your millions?" Holly asked.

"No idea," I said. "I've got enough money. It'll be nice to have more, I guess."

"You won't get a fancy new boat?"

"You know how much I love this old tub," I said. "I could never replace her. She's been my life for a long time now."

"What about a house?"

"Are you serious?" I asked. "Live on land? Never."

"Yea, me neither," she said. "I'll be rich but live just like I do now. I won't have to work, though."

"Maybe the hunt was more important than getting rich," I offered. "Gave us something to do with our time."

"I'm sure Shirley will be happy to be rich," she said. "Poor woman doesn't have a thing."

"She's got her boat," I said. "Just like we do. I wouldn't be surprised if she gave every penny to her kid."

"Really?" she asked. "I thought maybe she'd want a house, or at least a nicer boat."

"Her daughter gave her an outboard for her dinghy one time," I said. "She forced Shirl to take it. Shirl didn't want it. It was mounted on the dinghy, but she rowed anyway. That's how she is."

"Tough old bird."

"That will be you in fifty years," I said. "Biceps like a body builder. Same stinky bathing suit for weeks. Paint in your hair. Begging rum and cigarettes from passing sailors."

"And always looking for gold," she said. "Stealing scuttlebutt from ignorant tourists."

"Aarrgh!" I said.

"I can't wait to see her face when we lay a few million bucks in her lap," said Holly.

"If we can figure out how to turn it into cash," I said. "Haven't worked that out yet."

"Identify interested parties," she said. "Sell to the highest bidder."

"Somehow, I don't think it's that easy."

"Well, you better figure it out, mister," she said. "I ain't out here dodging sharks for nothing."

"Oh, I'll figure something out," I told her. "It's what I do."

"Find the bad guys. Figure something out. Get the money. Get the girl," she said. "You're like a dime store novel hero."

"I'm nothing more than a boat bum," I said. "The rest of that shit just happens. I'm certainly no hero."

"Shirley will think so," she said. "What was that accountant's name, Tom? He sure thought so when you saved his ass over in the Bahamas. Hell, Breeze, you're my hero too."

"Your hero? I asked. "Why?"

"You fixed my boat when it was wrecked," she said. "You went after Rabble when he robbed me. You showed me a whole world that I didn't know existed. You taught me to live, not just exist. You showed me that real men still exist. As rough as you are sometimes, you've shown me your heart. Definitely hero material."

"Aw shucks, ma'am," I said. "I never asked to be anybody's hero. I'm just trying to survive out here."

"Speaking of surviving," she said. "What do we do if that shark is still around?"

"The hero will wrestle him down, tie a rope to his tail, and water ski across the pass," I said.

"Seriously," she said. "I don't like the look in his eye."

"Let's hope he's gone."

Eleven

The morning sky was full of promise as we motored out of the bay and back to the search area. We were both anxious to bring up the rest of Shirley's gold. I anchored us over the spot and we both looked for any sign of our shark friend. We shared a nervous excitement. Some old pirate's hoard had been found. We were about to liberate it from its watery grave. We just needed to avoid its only guard, a ten-foot long, cantankerous hammerhead.

We sat for two hours. We saw no sharks. Slowly the lust for treasure overcame our fear of being eaten alive. Holly suited up. She wore a knife strapped to her left thigh. A spare light and the folding shovel hung from her belt. She adjusted her mask and gave me a thumbs up.

"Safety first, gold second," I told her.

"Keep your eyes open," she said. "Stay alert."

"Both times he's showed up was after we started disturbing the bottom," I said. "The prop wash cloud brought him in, and when you were digging."

"So I should be okay to go down and take a look," she said. "He comes when the muck starts flying."

"Seems that way," I agreed. "Go see what we're dealing with."

She was down for five minutes. I kept a sharp look-out. No sharks appeared. I didn't like the look on her face when she came back up. She was shaking her head back and forth. Something was wrong. She hung on the swim platform and asked for the metal detector.

"What's going on?" I asked.

"It's completely covered up," she said. "I can't even see where the trench was."

"The storm must have filled it in," I said. "Fuck."

"Hand me a small marker," she said. "I'll locate it again."

She went back down with the detector. A few minutes later the Gatorade bottle we used as a float popped to the surface. She'd found it.

She came to the top a few seconds later. She climbed aboard right away, instead of hanging in the water.

"I'm creeped out by that shark," she said. "I don't want to start digging around down there."

"If our theory is correct," I said. "He'll show up soon after we start excavating."

"What do we do?"

"I'll give it one shot," I said. "I wish we had a bang stick or some other way to protect ourselves."

"We can pick up one when we go for supplies," she said.

"Let's grab what we can before we give up. Give me your flippers and mask."

Holly was clearly spooked. I tried to remain calm. I acted like it was no big deal, pretending that I wasn't worried about the shark. I gave her a smile before sliding off the platform. I descended slowly, looking around in every direction. I followed the line from the float to the bottom. I tried parting the sand very carefully. If I could keep the cloudiness to a minimum, maybe the shark wouldn't know I was there. The sand kept falling back into the hole I had just made. I tried to recreate the trench, pulling the shovel along a straight line about four foot long. I went back over it, taking care not to stir up too much sediment. It was working, but progress was too slow. The sand was very loose and it just kept refilling the trench. My movements were awkward. I was a clumsy swimmer when I was doing it for fun. Working down there was like working on the moon. I reminded myself to keep calm. I slowed my breathing and concentrated on the task at hand. I kept clawing away with the little folding shovel.

I poked the shovel downward, trying to find metal. I worked it back and forth, pushing it deeper. Clink. I hit something, but it was still two feet under the sand. I put the shovel down and stuck my hand into what was left of the hole. I couldn't get to it. I was in the hole up to my elbow, trying to stretch my reach with my fingers. The gold was just beyond my grasp.

That's when I got steamrolled. I took a solid blow to my right side from what felt like a torpedo. I thought I heard a rib crack. The shark had clobbered me, which they sometimes do before taking a bite. Other than the rib, I was unhurt. I didn't panic. My first instinct was to burst to the surface, but I kept my cool. I slowly eased my arm out of the hole. I took a few deep breaths, then tossed the breather and hose away from me. I was hoping the bubble stream would distract him. *Go for the bubbles you dumb fish.*

I rose slowly. My ascent was almost imperceptible. *Stay calm, Breeze. Nice and slow.* I didn't want to flap my arms or kick my feet. I just floated. The shark had disappeared into the cloud I'd made while digging. I hadn't noticed how thick it had gotten. It was thick enough to wake up Mr. Hammerhead. He'd come running just as predicted. I watched him emerge from the cloud. He went for the bubbles. I went to the surface. At the last second, I gave a few hard kicks. I burst out of the water, onto the swim platform, and right into the boat in one not-so-smooth motion. My mask and flippers were all I had left.

Holly had a terrified look on her face.

"I never saw it," she said. "I'm so sorry. He didn't surface. I never saw him."

"Stay away from the side of the boat, but pull up the air hose," I said.

She wound the hose up. The shark flashed by as it came out of the water.

"The milk crate is down there too," I said, moving towards the line that held it.

She pulled up the crate. We got a good look at the creature's teeth as it approached the crate. It veered off at the last second, realizing that the plastic box wasn't food.

"Jesus, Breeze," said Holly. "Are you all right?"

"I think it broke my rib," I said. "Having a little trouble breathing right now. I lost the shovel."

"Screw that shovel," she said. "Let's get you inside."

I took off my wet swim trunks before I plopped myself on the couch. Holly brought me dry shorts and a towel.

"Can I get you anything?"

"Advil and rum," I said. "And a beer."

"That shark is bad juju," Holly said. "I don't see how we're going to get the rest of the gold with him around."

"Doesn't look too promising," I said. "The sand is too deep."

"Time for a new plan, Mr. Smart Guy."

"Let me drink on it," I said.

I couldn't wrap my head around being pummeled by a hammerhead shark. My side hurt like hell. I couldn't take deep breaths without suffering stabbing pain. I knew then why they called them hammerheads. I'd certainly been hammered. I took three Advil, chugged down a good slug of rum, and washed it all down with beer. I tried to get comfortable while Holly packed up our gear. The treasure was covered up. Our prop wash rig no longer existed. A freaking shark showed up every time we started digging. The situation was hopeless. Now I was hurt, further complicating matters.

On the positive side, we had a basket full of gold bars, and one little gold man. It was worth something. We hadn't totally struck out. It was just going to be so hard to leave the rest of it down there. We knew where it was, but we needed a much more serious recovery operation if we wanted to get it. We needed to regroup and come back with the proper equipment and expertise.

Holly came back to check on me.

"You're not looking so hot," she said. "Do we need to get you to a doctor?"

"A doctor won't do shit for a broken rib," I said. "Send me home with some pills maybe."

"You need some pills," she said. "I was told controlling the pain was the first priority for broken ribs."

"I've got rum and Advil," I said.

"You can't drink rum all day, every day," she said. "Ribs take weeks to heal."

"Let's go back to Marathon," I suggested. "Somebody will have some pills."

"You're a stubborn fool," she said. "Just go to the ER."

"I can't expose myself like that," I said. "They'll want all of my personal information. The FBI will be on me within hours."

"I guess you're right," she admitted. "We're going to have to figure out something on that front too."

"Lots of figuring out to do," I agreed.

"Such is the life you lead," she said. "Don't you ever consider stopping all this adventure?

Just settle down someplace nice? Live a normal, quiet life?"

"Do you?"

"I think maybe I am now," she said. "After we cash in."

"So your sailing wanderlust is over?" I asked. "We could have picked any number of peaceful islands in the Bahamas to settle down on."

"That's a conversation for another day," she said. "Right now we've got to decide what to do about our current situation. Do you want to call it quits? Sell what we've got?"

"Or find the right equipment," I said. "Maybe even someone who knows what they're doing."

"Bring in another partner?" she asked.

"Just thinking out loud," I answered. "We're clearly out of our league here."

"Where do we find someone?"

"Key West," I said. "That would be my first guess."

"You want to go back and talk to that Mel Fisher woman?" she asked.

"It's a place to start," I said. "We can poke around Boot Key on the way down."

"What about Shirley?"

"I guess we should pay her a visit," I said. "Let her know what we're up against."

"And how much we've recovered so far," she said. "Maybe she'll be happy with that."

"Except we don't know the value of the statue," I said. "Is it a fifty thousand dollar item? Or a million dollar item?"

"Good point," she said. "What do you want to do with the gold in the meantime?"

"Stash it below," I said. "Wrap it up in something. Cover it up with whatever you can find down there."

Holly knew her way around my boat's bilge. She'd helped me work down there enough. It had various hatches and compartments, some of which once held weed and coke. I heard her moving things around. I trusted that she'd hide our finds sufficiently. Smuggling gold was a new gig for me. Once you've run drugs and people, gold was about all there was left. I mentally added another item to my resume.

Holly finished stowing the gold.

"Do you want to get underway tonight?" she asked.

"Let me rest for now," I said. "This rib is killing me. We can wait until the morning if you don't mind."

"That will give me a chance to find that weed you told me about," she said, giggling.

"You'll never find it without me," I said. "The rangers never did."

"Rest up, then," she said. "You can show me in the morning before we leave."

I drank enough rum to ease the pain, then I drank a little more. I passed out sometime before dark. It didn't last. I kept waking up every hour or so. No position was comfortable. I gave up before daylight. I poked my head into Holly's bunk to check on her. Even with slobber running down her chin she was pretty. She had such a natural look, she didn't need to fuss about her skin or hair. She slept with no clothes on. Part of me wanted to climb into bed with her. The other part, a rib specifically, told me that it would be painful.

I turned on the coffee maker and went outside. I sat and looked at the dwindling stars. I heard dolphins nearby, but I couldn't see them. I loved that little place in the world more than ever. If I could get the FBI off my back, Holly and I could just live there, happily ever after. It would be smarter to leave the country, though. We also had two boats to worry about. Neither of us would want to give up our boat. Then there was the gold. I could live a very long time on the money I already had, maybe for the rest of my life. Holly could not. If we parted ways, she'd be looking for a job eventually. I hated to think of her cleaning boat bottoms for the rest of her life. I decided that we needed to dig up the rest of it, for Shirley, and for Holly. Everyone involved would be financially secure, whether Holly and I stayed together or not. My mind was made up.

I swallowed more Advil with my coffee. I snuck a shot of rum before Holly woke up. The pain in my side was slightly less sharp, but any wrong move set me on fire. I wouldn't be wrestling sharks anytime soon. Holly came out, rubbing the sleep out of her eyes.

"Good morning, glory," I said.

"I'm glad you're in one piece," she said. "I had a dream about that shark ripping you to shreds."

"I appreciate your concern," I said. "But apparently, I'm too bitter for his taste."

"I wouldn't want to test that theory," she said. "How are you feeling this morning?"

"A little better," I said.

"Up for a hike on the island?"

"I can check the first few plants," I said. "But if they're gone, I don't want to walk all over hell and gone looking for the others."

"Sweet," she said. "We've both been a little too tense lately."

"You're on your own," I said. "I haven't smoked dope since high school."

"Oh, come on, Breeze," she said. "It will do you good to mellow out some."

"I don't know," I said. "We'll see."

"It'll be fun," she said. "Let your hair down some."

After breakfast, we set out on a marijuana hunt. I had only my memory to rely on, and the foliage had grown and changed since I last tended those plants. The first spot was a bust. I found the row of stones I'd left to mark it, but there was nothing there. The second spot had the dried, dead stalk of a plant, but there was no green, no buds. The third plant hadn't survived either, but it had dropped some seeds in the soil around it. Two new plants had taken hold. They weren't real healthy looking, but there was enough there to pack a bowl or two. Holly bagged up a handful of leaves and tiny buds.

Back on the boat, she pulled a beer can out of the trash. She flattened one side, then used her knife to poke holes in the flat spot. She put one of the sad looking little buds on it, fired up a lighter, and inhaled through the opening in the can. She held it for a few seconds, then exhaled right into my face. It smelled sweet.

"Not bad," she said. "It's pretty smooth."

"I called it Island Smiles when I was selling it," I said. "Never smoked any of it."

"Here," she said, handing me the beer can.

With anyone else, I would have said no. I remembered the paranoia from my youth. I didn't want to lose control of my faculties. I needed to stay alert, but when she handed me the can, I just took it. She held the lighter on the dope and I inhaled. It tasted as sweet as it smelled. Like she had done, I held it for a few seconds before exhaling. We moved to the back deck, sat down, and took in our surroundings. Within a few minutes, I was indeed mellow. The colors were a little brighter. I forgot about the pain in my side. I didn't feel drunk or dopey, just relaxed.

"You okay?" asked Holly.

"I'm good," I responded. "Just a little high."

For some reason, that was hilarious to her. She laughed and cackled at my expense. I didn't see what was so funny, but her laugh was infectious. Before I knew it, I was laughing too.

"Breeze is high," she said. "I'd never thought I'd see the day. You're the last person I ever thought would smoke dope."

"Then why'd you make me do it?" I asked.

"I didn't make you do shit," she said. "You took it willingly."

"I was influenced," I said. "And now I'm under the influence."

That was hilarious too. We broke out into a laughing fit again. It was silly, but I really didn't care. I didn't care about the gold, my busted rib, or solving any of our problems. I just was. I sat there smiling. I looked at the water. I looked at Holly. It was all good. Then I got sleepy.

"I feel like I need a nap," I said. "But we should get underway. Daylight's wasting."

"Help me get the anchor up," she said. "I'll take us out of the Pass. You can take a nap. Some party animal you are."

I had no pithy reply. I was getting a little foggy. I straightened up and went forward to raise the anchor. Holly took the helm. After we got underway, I stuck my head up on the bridge.

"I'm going to lay down," I said. "Wake me up if you need me."

"Sweet dreams," she said. "I'll be fine."

I was almost instantly asleep. The gentle rocking of the boat and the buzz I had, combined to pull me down into unconsciousness. We'd been keeping a vigorous schedule. I was injured. My body needed rest. Smoking with Holly had turned out to be good medicine. I slept deeply. When I woke, I felt a lot better, and I was really hungry. I made a peanut butter and jelly sandwich, grabbed a bag of chips and a Gatorade, and joined Holly on the bridge.

"Where are we?" I asked.

"South of Fort Myers Beach," she said. "Do you want to go out around the shoals or into Marco?"

"When's the high tide at Marco?" I asked.

"Looks like we'll get there about an hour before the high," she said.

"Perfect," I said. "We can take the back way to Goodland. Check in on Shirley."

It was near sundown when we reached Capri Pass. I didn't want to run the tricky inland route to Goodland in the dark. We motored past The Snook Inn and turned out of the channel to drop anchor in Factory Bay. The ache in my side had returned. I opted not to smoke my way out of pain again. I turned to rum and Advil instead. At the rate I was going, we'd need to restock the rum locker pretty soon. I hadn't been hurt like that in a long time. I didn't like it much. Holly kept asking what she could do to help, but there wasn't anything she could do to ease the pain. She smoked the rest of her meager weed supply while I alternated between beer and rum.

"What about that damn shark?" she asked.

"What about him?"

"How are we going to work in the water with him around?"

"I suppose we could catch him," I suggested.

"You don't have the right tackle," she said.

"We can get some," I said. "Big stiff rod. Heavy reel. Strong line. Big ass hooks."

"What do we do with him if we catch him?"

"If we keep him tied up long enough," I said. "He'll die."

"Is that legal?"

"I don't think so."

"Hmm," she said, fiddling with her phone.

"What do you have?" I asked. "What does Google say?"

"It's illegal to kill a hammerhead shark," she answered. "Has been since 2012. They must be released unharmed, immediately."

"As we smoke dope and take artifacts from state waters without notifying the Florida authorities," I said.

"Not the same," she said. "Those are victimless crimes."

"Hard to see that shark as a victim," I said.

"True, but it is a living thing."

"So we either tie him off, trying to keep him alive," I said. "Or we drag him twenty miles out to sea."

"He could just swim back, couldn't he?"

"Probably," I said. "He seemed territorial."

"Two boats," I said. "And another person. We hook the bastard, drag him out to sea. While he's being taken away, the underwater work gets done. We release him way out there someplace. If he heads straight back, the work is already done when he arrives."

"I can see that," she said. "But again, it means bringing in another partner. That could create problems of a different kind."

"We'll work a deal with someone," I said. "Just hire them for a job, not a cut of the take."

"Any number of people can catch a fish," she said. "What about your buddies in Fort Myers Beach?"

"Robin and Diver Dan?" I asked. "Sure they could catch him, but we need a treasure boat. One that's already rigged up with decent gear."

"We could put a better rig on your boat," she suggested. "Robin or Dan can use their own boat to haul the shark out in the Gulf."

"I'm not going to be much help with the physical labor," I said. "I'm a handicap until this rib heals."

"So we search the Keys for someone who has the right kind of boat and equipment, that they don't happen to be using at the moment," she said. "Seems like a long shot."

"This is Florida," I said. "There has to be an idle treasure hunting boat somewhere."

"It's a hundred miles from Key West to Key Largo," she said. "Probably a hundred marinas and boatyards in between."

"We ask people," I said. "We gather intel. We keep our eyes and ears open."

"Great," she said. "A mission within a mission."

"It'll work out," I said. "Shit always works out."

"You keep telling me that."

Twelve

We found Shirley sitting on her boat the next day. She was wearing the same bathing suit we'd seen her in the last time we'd visited. She'd finished her topside paint job. She was using a putty knife to dig out one of the flies she'd painted over.

"Damn flies," she said. "As soon as you put down white paint, they land in it. Serves them right to get painted over."

She scratched her nose with the paintbrush still in her hand. A white streak appeared under the bill of her hat. She didn't seem to notice.

"Did you bring me any smokes?" she asked. "I got a bottle of cheap rum, but you can't find smokes in this one-horse town."

"Sorry," I said. "We haven't been to town. You don't have to buy cheap booze anymore Shirl. You've got twenty grand."

"Expensive rum ain't no better than the cheap stuff," she said. "Fancy liquor is a waste of money."

"We've got some news," I said.

"Is it good or bad?" she asked.

I proceeded to explain what we'd been through and what we'd found. I told her about the intrinsic but unknown value of the statue. The value of the bars was tied to the value of the little gold man. If there was some great historical relevance to the whole collection, it would be worth many times more than just selling the bars for their gold value.

"How many of them bars have you got?" she asked.

"Eleven," I said. "You gave us two. We found ten more, but we sort of lost one."

"He gave it away," Holly chimed in. "But it was the only way to get us out of a jam."

"Trouble?" asked Shirley.

"We had to run some pirates off," I told her. "But I think we've seen the last of them."

"Is that all there is?" she asked.

"We think there're another forty or so bars," I said. "And a few more figurines."

"Why didn't you bring up the rest of it?" she asked.

"Equipment failure, storms, shark attack," I said. "We're lucky we got anything at all, the way everything went wrong for us."

"Now what?" she asked. "You just gonna leave it down there?"

"We hope to find a proper treasure recovery boat," I said. "Go back and sweep the place clean."

"I want to go with you," she said. "I'm bored out of my gourd here. Only so many times I can go to the Little Bar."

"We're going to the Keys first," I said. "Hopefully, we'll come back with what we need to get the job done."

"I'd just like to be on that boat when a big old pile of gold comes up," she said. "That would tickle me pink. I've dreamt about it my whole life."

"Give Holly your phone number," I said. "We'll let you know when we're on our way."

"I'll meet you in Pelican Bay," she said. "Don't start digging without me."

There was no reason she couldn't come along. She already owned half of whatever we might recover. I looked forward to seeing her face when we finally brought up the rest of it. At least we knew she didn't want to cash out yet. She was in for the big score.

We left for Marathon that same day. I drove the boat until happy hour. Holly took over so I could drink some painkilling medicine. After a healthy slug of rum and a couple beers, I felt better. We snuck into Boot Key Harbor after dark. We anchored just inside the bridge for the night. We'd move to a marina in the morning. The boat had a new name and a new look, but there was no point in advertising that we'd arrived. We snuck around in the dark with the dinghy. I wanted to see if Rabble's boat was in the harbor. It was not on a mooring ball. It was not anchored near Dockside. We did see Rogue anchored there, but no Rabble. Unless he was in the creek, he wasn't around.

We tucked into Marathon Marina the next morning. Holly went off to find me some pills, and to check on her boat. I went to Castaway's Bar to start my inquiries into treasure hunters. I went to Burdine's too. I walked across US 1 to the docks that held fishing and dive boats. I learned nothing. I got funny looks. I met back up with Holly at the marina. She'd found me a bottle of Oxyco-done. I popped two of them and plopped my tired ass down.

"Nothing much going on here," I said. "We should probably go to Key West. We can talk to the Mel Fisher people. Look around the docks."

"You want to take a boat or a bus?" she asked.

"I hate anchoring down there," I said. "And a slip costs as much as a hotel room."

"Bus it is," she said.

Before we left, Holly laid out all the gold bars and the little gold man. She used her cell phone to take pictures of our stash. We wouldn't have to carry any of it on the bus. We made an appointment to speak with the director. She was waiting for us when we arrived. She was very curious about what we'd found, and where we'd found it. She looked through the pictures with great interest.

"As I explained to you before," she said. "We are not in business to purchase pieces of gold, even a lone figurine."

"Right," I said. "You're in business to find them yourselves. That's what you do."

"Correct," she said. "We are prepared to make you a significant offer for the location of your site. If you sign a contract with us, we'd purchase what you already have, to make the collection complete. But, it would be our collection, our find. You'd have to sign a non-disclosure agreement."

"Why would I do that?" I asked.

"We'd make a nice offer, Mr. Breeze," she said. "You have to understand a few things. We know that there are significant troves out there, yet to be discovered. We have people scouring the Spanish archives constantly. That's how Mr. Fisher found the Atocha. It's likely that we could identify the source of your gold through our research. It would be a boon to the future viability of our recovery business. An incentive to our investors. There would be a documentary made, books written. The whole nine yards. It would have great historical significance."

"Millions of dollars," I said. "But only a tiny percentage for me and my crew."

"The greater good belongs to the world," she said. "Not to some rich collector that you may or may not be able to sell it to."

"Maybe hundreds of millions," I continued. "What kind of offer would cause me to give up on that kind of money?"

"One hundred thousand for the gold," she said. "Another hundred thousand for the exact coordinates and other relevant information. Depth, current, hazards."

"I don't think so," I said. "Holly, give her your phone number. When she starts talking seven figures I may reconsider."

"How will you sell your gold, Mr. Breeze?" the director asked.

"I'll pay you to give me the contacts I need," I said. "How's that for turning the tables?"

"You really don't want to go that route," she warned. "It's a dangerous path."

"Do you have the contacts?"

"I might," she said. "But not for the actual buyers. There are certain individuals, I guess you could call them brokers. They're known to the major artifact traders."

"I tell you what," I said. "You chew on that piss poor offer you made me. I'll go get the rest of the gold and statues. We'll meet again. See what happens."

"It's worthless to us if we don't find it," she said. "Or at least claim to have found it."

"Then think of a price tag for the contact information of those brokers," I said. "Have a nice day."

I walked out and Holly followed. We started walking towards Duval Street. I was ready for a drink.

"Two hundred grand?" said Holly. "That would give Shirley one hundred. We'd each get fifty."

"There's two million laying there," I said. "Maybe twenty million."

"What next?"

"We find us a treasure hunter," I said.

We spent three days kicking around the docks. The Key West Bight was home to the sunset cruise boats, day sailors, and fancy yachts renting expensive slips. It was also home to the infamous dinghy dock, which supported all the liveaboards that anchored in the harbor. We spoke to several of them. They were a motley bunch, ranging from the drug addicted to the criminally insane. Some were just service workers in town. They were bartenders and waitresses, working hard to live in paradise. None of them knew anything about treasure boats or treasure hunters, except for the black cowboy.

His name was Kenyatta. He wore pointy-toed cowboy boots, a rhinestone-encrusted vest, and a bandana around his neck. He had a guitar hanging on his back.

"You need to find Tommy Thompson," he said. "Knows more about finding gold than any man alive."

"Who's Tommy Thompson?" I asked.

"You don't know?" he said. "Then you don't know about no treasure hunting. Aside from Mr. Mel Fisher, Tommy's the most famous of them all."

"I guess I don't know much, really," I said. "Strictly an amateur."

"I doubt Tommy would waste his time then," he said.

"Where can I find him?" I asked.

"Lord only knows," he said. "He hid from the Feds for years. Last I knew he was up in Key Largo."

"Hid from the Feds?"

"You need to read on Mr. Thompson," he said. "I've got to get down to Mallory."

"Thanks, Kenyatta."

We walked over to the raw bar and used Holly's phone to look up Tommy Thompson. His story was incredible. He invented his own device, which he called Nemo. He used it to locate the long lost S.S. Central America, off the coast of South Carolina. The ship had gone down in 1857 during a hurricane. Many had searched for it, but none ever succeeded, until Tommy. He recovered the ship's bell, two gold coins, and one bar. He showed that to nearly one hundred investors in the fall of 1988. He asked them to keep it quiet, and, amazingly, they did.

It took him a few years, cost him his marriage, but eventually he built an even better Nemo. He began hauling up large quantities of gold. He was immediately beset by legal problems. A bunch of insurance companies sued him. They claimed to have insured the ship in the

1800's. When he sold a portion of the gold for a reported fifty million dollars, his investors claimed they never saw any profits. Tommy Thompson disappeared. He became invisible. A warrant was issued for his arrest in 2012 after he failed to appear in court.

They lived off the radar in a Florida mansion for six years. They paid rent with damp cash that had been buried underground. Tommy had a dozen different cell phones, all acquired with false identities. When a handyman recognizes Tommy and his girlfriend, the pair fled with just a few belongings, and cash. They stayed hidden in a West Palm Beach hotel, until recently. Both were jailed until Tommy would give up the location of the missing gold. The state and his original investors took it all. Unless there was a secret stash hidden away somewhere else, Tommy was broke. That's where the trail ended. There was no mention of him living in Key Largo, or anywhere else. How would the black cowboy know where he was? Who knew in the Keys? The Coconut Telegraph was a powerful communication system.

We decided to walk down to Mallory Square ourselves, to catch the sunset. The first street performer we saw was putting his entire body through a tennis racket with no strings. We walked on to see the guy on a giant unicycle telling jokes. We checked out the vendors with their homemade crafts, paintings, and sunset photographs. We joined in applause as the sun set. As we were leaving the square, we saw the black cowboy. He was wailing on his guitar. He wasn't a cowboy, after all, he was the Key West Jimi Hendrix. He had a good crowd gathered. I tossed a ten dollar bill in his guitar case. He nodded in thanks.

"Do you think this Tommy Thompson is a good lead?" asked Holly.

"I don't know," I admitted. "We'll work our way up the Keys. If we don't find someone, we'll try to find him in Key Largo."

We asked around in Garrison Bight the next day. This was more of a working harbor, with fishing boats and assorted watermen tied up everywhere. It also included Houseboat Row. These weren't really boats at all, just houses that happened to float. Most of them were rentals. There was no one around with any useful knowledge. A lobsterman told us that the only working treasure boats in Key West belonged to the Mel Fisher operation. They mostly took tourists out to the wreck sites. They'd seed the wrecks with a gold coin or two for the tourists to find. He said he'd heard of a few small time operations further up the coast but had no first-hand knowledge.

Our last stop was Stock Island. It was a hard place, compared to downtown Key West. There were plenty of work boats at the various docks and boatyards. There were plenty of derelict boats too. We had lunch at the Hog Fish and spoke with the bartender. She looked like she'd been around the block a few times.

"Every gold hunting fool in the country was down here after the Atocha was found," she said. "But that craze died off pretty quick. Haven't seen a treasure boat in years."

"Any guys still around that used to work one of those boats?" I asked.

"There's a couple," she said. "But let me tell you, mister, they're hopeless drunks or addicts. Won't be of any use to you."

We walked the docks. Most of the boats were set up to pull lobster traps. A couple of rusted out shrimp trawlers listed against the seawall. The men we saw were hard cases, with alligator skin and prison tattoos. Some of them catcalled Holly. I was uncomfortable. Normally, I could handle myself, but my broken rib left me vulnerable. I couldn't risk a fight. We made our way back to the nearest bus stop and left town.

Thirteen

We spent another week checking out the docks and marinas of the lower Keys. We poked around Boca Chita, Summerland, Ram Rod, Big Pine and the Saddlebunch Keys. We talked to boat owners, fishermen, barmaids and old men in tackle shops. The treasure hunter was extinct. He didn't exist in the lower Keys. If he did, he wasn't telling anyone. We were looking for Sasquatch in the sub-tropics.

We regrouped back in Marathon. Holly and I sat on my boat and discussed alternatives. We wondered if, with a little research, we could outfit a boat on our own. What did we need? How did it work? What did it cost? How long would it take? We also learned that we were supposed to apply for an Exploration and Recovery Permit. The process was restrictive. The state of Florida believed that anything found in its waters belonged to the state. Mel Fisher had a lot of trouble fighting the state in court, but things had gotten worse since his day.

We'd already assumed our entire operation was illegal, so we didn't sweat it. I had never been one to cower over stepping over the legal line. I didn't want to break the law, but some laws were just stupid. Finders Keepers didn't apply to sunken treasure in Florida? Ridiculous. Buying a boat and outfitting it with proper recovery equipment would take too long, and cost too much. It was a last resort. We knew that with the right gear, we'd have the rest of the gold in a day or two. Neither of us wanted to waste months of time, but we were also wasting time looking for help.

We went up to Islamorada to poke around. Bud n Mary's was the center of the universe as far as boats go. We met a charter captain, who told us about a guy, who knew a guy, who might know another guy. We ran around in circles, chasing a ghost until we met John Kipp. John had worked on a gold boat back in the eighties for a few months. He wore a big gold medallion around his neck and a gray ponytail. He had the leather skin and squinted eyes of a man who had spent a lifetime on the water. He was a fly fishing guide now, out of the Lorelei. Back in the seventies, he and his buddy Sonny had ruled the guiding roost from Islamorada to Flamingo. Sonny switched from being a light tackle guide to running offshore charters. He hated the fishing out there, but he liked the paydays that came with running dope in from offshore.

"It was part of the culture back then," said John. "No one thought it was doing any harm. Most of us picked up a bale or two when the fishing was slow."

"I know a bit about it myself," I told him.

"Run some dope, have you?" he asked.

"For Bald Mark," I said. "You know him?"

"Heard of him," he said. "Wouldn't ever work for him."

"Wise choice," I said.

"I thought he was like the mafia," he said. "Once you were in, you couldn't get out."

"Remember hearing about him going to jail?" I asked. "I ran all of his dope while he was in prison, with the condition that I could leave his operation when he got out."

"And here you are," he said. "Looking for gold."

"Which led me to you," I said. "Do you still know anyone with a boat or the expertise that could help us out?"

"Tommy Thompson is out of jail now," he said. "He's been working on one of his old boats for a month now."

"You know him?"

"I sell him some weed," he said. "Talk fishing. Yearn for the old days. Jail didn't do him no good."

"He's in Key Largo?"

"He's got a dock at his mom's place, up by Angelfish Creek," he said. "He pulled a rust bucket out of the mangroves and tied it off there. Still got all the gear, but it's in bad shape."

"He's still got the itch for gold," I said.

"Must have," he said. "Or he wouldn't be wasting his time. That rig needs a lot of work."

"Maybe he's got a pile of coins hidden somewhere," I said. "He just needs it to work long enough to bring them up."

"He'd never be able to sell them," he said. "He's a marked man when it comes to gold."

"He could use a third-party," I said. "Someone he trusts."

"If you're hinting at me," he said. "You're barking up the wrong tree."

"Just thinking," I said. "You think he'd be willing to help us?"

"Help you what?"

"Pull up a pile of gold," I told him.

"Can't speak for him," he said.

"Can you tell me how to find him?

"Best not," he said. "But I could take you to him. I'll run my boat through the mangroves and flats so you won't be able to trace your way back."

"Fair enough," I said. "Your introduction would help too."

"Hard to say," he said. "He ain't what he used to be. Before he went to jail, he was probably the smartest man in Florida. Can't say that anymore. He's lost everything, including half his mind."

"When can we go?"

"Meet at the ramp behind the Lorelei tomorrow at ten," he said. "It'll take us an hour to get up to his place."

"Thanks, John."

I decided to have Holly come along to meet Tommy. Having a cute, young chick around couldn't hurt. We met John Kipp at the ramp.

"I talked to Tommy last night," John said. "He's skeptical, but he doesn't have much else to do, so he'll listen to you."

"Any suggestions on how to handle him?" I asked.

"He's had the gold fever for forty years," he said. "Stick with the gold."

"That's what we came for," I said.

John ran his flats boat like most backcountry guides, flat out. He kept the throttle pinned as we swerved between grass flats and oyster bars. We slowed in Tarpon Basin, as he took us into a low tunnel of mangroves. It didn't seem big enough for a kayak, but we squeezed through. He cut across the main channel on the other side and steered us around a dozen small islands. I had a good feel for where we were. We hit open water in Blackwater Sound and I knew for sure. John was taking us on an unnecessarily complicated route to try to throw us off. I knew more about the area than he thought, though.

We shot through a hole between Pumpkin Key and North Key Largo at sixty miles per hour. We came down off plane as John eased back on the throttle. He aimed us up a little creek, where we found an old shrimper tied up to a residential dock. A man onboard was welding a piece of steel at the base of an outrigger. When we pulled up, he stopped and tilted his welding mask up.

"John," he said.

"Tommy," said John. "This is the couple we spoke about."

"Come on aboard," he said.

He had unkempt curly dark hair sticking out all over the place. His beard was equally wild. His eyes were set deep under heavy brows. His clothes were a size too big, like he'd lost weight. He was almost six feet tall, but he stayed bent at the waist, making him appear shorter. He tilted his head up to look at us.

He put down the torch and took off his gloves and gear. I saw that he'd been strengthening the base of the outrigger to handle more load, or repair a broken weld. Instead of the blocks and tackle of a normal shrimper, he had installed an electric winch at the peak of the rigger's tower. Heavy steel cable ran down to a massive hook.

"Looks like you want to pick up something heavy," I said.

"Don't take a genius to figure that out," he replied.

"My name's Breeze," I said. "This is Holly."

"Nice to meet you, Mr. Thompson," said Holly.

"Tommy is fine," he said. "You're a sweet young thing."

"She's a first class diver," I told him. "And my partner."

"Just the two of you in this thing?" he asked. "The less the better."

"We've got an eighty-year-old lady that got this whole thing started," I said. "She'd like to observe. She's pretty salty. Good diver herself back in the day."

"She tip you to the spot?" she asked.

"That's right," I said. "Half is hers."

"How much is mine?"

"We hoped to hire you to do a job," I told him. "Not give you a percentage."

"It's not enough," he said.

"We'll pay you a fair amount to hire the boat," I said. "And we'll give you a fair wage to help us with our recovery. There is no search. There is no doubt. We just show up and grab the stuff. Simple as that."

"If it was that simple, you wouldn't need me," he said.

"It's buried under four feet of sand," I said. "Lots of current, and a mean shark."

"What water depth?"

"Ten feet."

"Bull shark?"

"Hammerhead."

"We'll have to take him out if he's still around," Tommy said.

"So you'll do it?" I asked.

"Not so fast," he said. "Whatever you think is fair to pay me, I don't care about that. I need a little help myself."

"You'll help us if we help you."

"Same kind of job," he said.

"You hid the rest of your gold under water," I said.

"A little deeper," he said. "No sharks as far as I know."

"How will you sell it?"

"How you going to sell yours?" he asked. "You must have a buyer in mind."

"Still working on that," I admitted.

The hard part ain't finding it," he said. "The hard part is making money off it, without anybody knowing."

"I'm hoping to make some contacts through the director at the Mel Fisher Museum," I said.

"She tried to buy you off, didn't she?"

"Yup. Didn't bite," I said. "But she seemed willing to take a payment to help me find potential buyers."

"It's just gold," he said. "Melt it down."

"It's more than that," I told him. "Little gold men. Idols, gods, figurines. Aztec maybe."

"Don't find that on the east coast," he said. "What I got is coins and bars, gold and silver of each."

"Different kind of buyer," I said.

"The kind of people you're looking for," he said. "They'd just as soon kill you and take what you got."

"You're not the first to say that," I said. "What about your gold? How do you plan to get rid of it?"

"I can't personally," he said. "But I know the players. I need a broker of my own."

"Do you know any of these artifact buyers?"

"Maybe," he said. "But I'm dead to all of them. Wouldn't know how to find them now. Don't know that I'd want them to find me either."

Holly interjected.

"If you want us to help you get your gold, and help you sell it," she said. "You'll have to help us sell ours too."

"That might sound fair to you," he said. "But I'm the one with the boat and the skill. You're the ones come looking for a favor."

"You help us get our gold," I said. "We'll help you get yours. That would be even. If we sell yours, you help sell ours. Again, even."

"This came at me pretty fast," he said. "I'm not finished with this boat yet. I'm going to need a few days."

"Can we come back without John?" I asked.

"If you think you can find your way," he said.

"No problem," I said.

"I'll let him know he didn't fool you none," he said.

"Let him think he did," I said. "The fewer people involved the better, right?"

He nodded in agreement.

John ran us back to Islamorada at the same speed, only slightly altering his route. We shook hands and I thanked him. He told me he didn't need to know the content of my conversation with Tommy. The less he knew the better. I offered him some gas money, but he declined.

I let Tommy chew on things for two full days. Holly and I moved *Freedom* up to Pumpkin Key. It was a short dinghy ride to Tommy's shrimper. During our first meeting, I'd concentrated on the man himself. I tried to gauge his motives, his abilities, and his trustworthiness. The jury was still out on his character. During the second meeting, I paid special attention to the boat itself. Tommy must have worked around the clock since we'd last seen him. A commercial generator had been bolted to the roof of the main cabin. To the left of the rear cabin door stood a huge air compressor. A hose reel was attached to the port side gunnel. It held a four-inch diameter hose of at least a hundred feet in length. Next to it was a rake of attachments, like you'd find on a vacuum cleaner, only bigger.

"If you use just the open hose," Tommy said. "You'll blow a big hole as deep as you want. These attachments allow a diver to control the flow. This handle here adjusts pressure and outflow. You'll be able to write your name on the bottom if you want to."

Although the outer hull of the converted shrimper was covered in rust, the decks and interior had been cleaned up and painted. The added equipment looked new. Tommy took me down in the engine room. It was spotless. The engine was freshly painted.

"That's a CAT 3208," he said. "Rebuilt her myself. We'll get ten knots if we need it. Hard on fuel."

"My boat only makes seven knots," I said. "Fast enough for me."

"Well good, then," he said. "Because she holds a thousand gallons of diesel. Not that we need that much, but we'll have to talk expenses."

"It's a little over three hundred miles, roundtrip, to my spot," I said. "Plus working time and generator fuel. I'll cover our part of the expedition. How far is your spot?"

"Not far," he said. "That's why I'm docked here, but I'm tapped out after all the work I've put into this tub."

"How were you going to buy fuel if I hadn't shown up?"

"I don't know," he admitted. "I just figured something would come along. You know, shit works out and all. Got right down to it, I'd steal fuel ten gallons at a time if I had to."

"Tough to get investors I'll bet, after your track record."

"There's that," he said.

"How much gold do you have out there, Tommy?" I asked.

"Enough to pay those bastards back," he said. "With plenty left over for me."

"What do you owe them?"

"Judge figured a little over twelve million," he said.

"Why did you do it?"

"I ask myself daily," he said. "Just to run for the sake of running I suppose. I had the money. I had the smarts. I just said fuck it all and took off. Took them six years to catch up to me."

I thought about my own story. I'd done the same thing. I'd taken the money, said fuck it all, and ran. I knew it was wrong, but I'd done it anyway. My wife's death has started it all. I didn't cope. I couldn't cope. I wanted to hide from it all. That's why I had done it. I remembered reading something about Tommy's wife leaving him while he was hunting his treasure. Maybe that's what caused him to snap. Or maybe he just thought he was smart enough to get away with it.

I thought I'd been smart. Hell, I was invisible for a few years, but I got caught too. Fortunately, by the time it all fell apart for me, I had the money to make amends. Now Tommy needed to make his own amends. I'd help him get the money, right after he helped me get mine. I said a silent thanks to the black cowboy in Key West. I'd never hear a Jimi Hendrix song again without thinking of him.

Tommy spent some time showing Holly how the compressor, hoses, and attachments worked. He'd rigged a mesh basket to the outrigger and connected it to the electric winch. Once we positioned the boat over our target, she'd go down with the hose. It would be easy work clearing the sand with Tommy's rig. She'd toss the gold bars and whatever else she found into the basket. Tommy would haul it up. That's all there was to it, except for the shark.

I'd gotten a good, strong offshore fishing rod back at Bud n Mary's. The staff helped me put together the right reel, line, leaders, and hooks to fight a big shark. I was confident I could catch him, but we still hadn't decided what to do with him once he was hooked. Tommy came up with a surprisingly simple solution.

"You've see *Deadliest Catch*, right?" he asked. "They got them big holds to stuff all the crabs into. This here shrimper has the same thing."

"How do we get a ten-foot shark into the hold?" asked Holly.

"Winch 'em," he said, pointing up at the outrigger. "Put a tow rope on his tail. Drag him right up over the gunnels and drop him in the hold."

"Sharks need to swim to keep water moving over their gills," I said. "He'll die in there."

"I'll beef up the pumps," he said. "We can push water past him faster than he can breathe."

"Might work," I said.

"And we'll know right where he is the whole time we're working," he said.

"I like it," Holly said. "It's worth a try."

The plan was coming together. We ran the rusty old shrimper down to Gilbert's to take on fuel. The engine ran smoothly. Tommy smiled. I made the attendant stop at one thousand dollars. I frowned. We used Tommy's mother's car to buy groceries. We filled the fresh water tanks from her garden hose. We worked out which boats would be used and which would be left behind. Tommy's boat was too sparse inside for all of us to sleep on. He'd made a bunk for himself and that's it. The galley was limited to a two-burner camp stove and a dorm-room sized fridge. Of course, Holly wanted to sail *Another Adventure*. I did not want to leave my boat anywhere unattended. Her boat was safe in Boot Key Harbor. I won the argument. Holly and I would take my boat, while Tommy drove the shrimper by himself. Shirley would meet us there. We'd all have a party when the gold came up from the depths.

Fourteen

We all motored down the ICW until we picked up the old yacht channel across Florida Bay. I led the way. The big shrimper had a deeper draft than I did. We left the hold empty to reduce his draft. I radioed trouble spots back to Tommy as I crossed them. We rounded Cape Sable late in the afternoon, taking caution to avoid the shoals. We dropped anchor outside the Little Shark River for the night. We couldn't run all night long because Tommy was by himself.

We went over to his boat to talk strategy, and drink a few beers.

"We're going to need one more stop," I said. "Can't make it from here without losing daylight."

"This is your turf," he said. "You tell me."

I pulled out a chart and thought a minute. Normally, I'd stop at Fort Myers Beach, but I had to be mindful of the FBI. Tommy's boat was too big for a mooring ball anyway. I pointed to a stretch of water between the Sanibel Causeway and Point Ybel.

"Along here," I said. "Go far enough in to get out of the weather. The current is strong, so put down a good hook."

We left at first light. I angled in close to shore near Marco so Holly could get a cell signal. She called Shirley. Shirley had already made her way up to Pelican Bay. She was anchored inside and wondering what was taking us so long. Holly told her to keep her pants on. We'd be there in two days. We arrived off Point Ybel late in the afternoon. Again, we adjourned to discuss details.

"I'm going to anchor over the spot first," I told Tommy. "I've got a good mark on it. Holly will go down with the metal detector and place a heavy buoy for you to see. We'll back off and you come in after us."

"Aye," he said. "Sounds simple enough."

Anchoring over an exact spot is a tricky business. It's rarely exact. You take current and wind into account, drop anchor and let out scope, hoping to hit the target. We'd used stern anchors to swing the back of the boat over our target, which had actually worked pretty well. With Tommy's rig, we didn't need to be perfect. He had a hundred feet of hose for Holly to use. We just needed him to get close enough. So far, he seemed a capable captain.

We made the Boca Grande Pass in the early afternoon. The tide was coming in. It carried us at a rapid clip past the old lighthouse and into Charlotte Harbor. I saw no fishing boats near the area we wanted to work. The sheepshead must have moved on. I did see Shirl. She was anchored near the spot we'd run aground on when we dragged in the storm. Her little boat only drew two feet of water. She was tucked in pretty close to shore, out of our way.

Tommy hovered nearby as I lined up the GPS mark. I called him on the radio, telling him to anchor. It would take a bit for Holly to mark the treasure. He went out deeper and dropped a short hook. I dropped mine and backed up until I was very near the spot. The current was still ripping in. I made Holly use a safety line, much to her objection.

"Don't dig around," I said. "You'll bring the shark in too soon. Just find it and drop the buoy."

She went down with the detector. I lowered the anchor with its attached float. It didn't take her long. We'd been over this spot several times already. We knew where the treasure was. I watched as the buoy moved. Holly was carrying the anchor to the spot she'd located with the detector. Eventually, she surfaced and gave me a thumbs up. No sharks interfered.

I moved to the bow and raised the anchor. I gave Tommy a wave. He pulled his and started our way. So far so good. I went over near Shirley's boat to re-anchor. I couldn't get in as far as she was, but I just wanted to make it easier for her to join us. She rowed over as soon as we got settled.

"Where'd you find that sad looking hulk?" she asked, pointing to Tommy's shrimper.

"Key Largo," I said. "Wait till you see her sad looking captain."

"Did you resurrect Mel Fisher himself to run that thing?"

"Close," I said. "You ever heard of Tommy Thompson?"

"Anyone who's ever thought about hunting for gold has heard of him," she said. "And you ain't got him because he's in jail. You got some imposter."

"I don't think so," I said. "If so, he's a damn good actor. Plus the boat is rigged to find gold."

"What are you paying him?

"Favors," I said. "When we leave here we'll have another pile to recover somewhere in the Keys."

"I knew it," she said. "That rat bastard stashed the rest of it someplace."

"He wants to repay the investors he ripped off," I told her. "But he says there's plenty more after that."

"Son of a bitch," she said. "Tommy damn Thompson. You never cease to amaze me, Breeze."

"Me either," said Holly. "He sets his mind to something, then stumbles around until it happens. It's a weird gift."

"You'd do well to learn from him," said Shirley. "For as long as you're around anyway."

Holly looked at me, questioning. Was I keeping her around? Was she keeping me around? Those were questions for another day.

"Let's go catch a shark," I said. "Tommy's lined up over there."

We loaded up the dinghy with fishing gear and a cooler. I had several big pieces of beef on ice. Holly had fashioned a fighting belt. We didn't have a fighting chair, so we'd have to improvise. We introduced Shirl to Tommy once aboard the shrimper.

The crew that I'd assembled was a motley one. Shirl was well over eighty. Her pacemaker and indomitable spirit kept her going long after most grandmothers took up knitting. Tommy was in his sixties, and worse for the wear. He paid no attention to grooming or hygiene. His head was always tilted down, like a dog that had been beaten too many times. Both of them had been chasing gold for a lifetime. Both of them had trusted me with their finds.

Holly was only in her very young thirties. She was nimble and quick. She was a sharp thinker, fast learner, fearless diver and sailor. We had been together, and we'd been apart, several times over. Whatever the status of our relationship, we trusted each other. A big moment was just in front of us. First, we had a shark to tackle.

Tommy set me up in a sturdy deck chair on the aft deck. Holly's jury-rigged harness had a webbed pocket for the rod butt. I ran a big ass stainless hook through a slab of bloody beef and left it drift away in the current, feeding out line as the meat disappeared beneath the surface. Tommy stood over my left shoulder. Holly stood on my right side. They were there to grab onto me if the fight got too intense. We sat and soaked the meat for thirty minutes. Nothing happened. Was the shark gone? Did he not like the smell of blood and beef?

We changed up baits to put some more blood in the water. Another thirty minutes passed without a bump.

"We need to blow some sand around," I said.

"Huh?" said Tommy.

"Every time we disturb the bottom, he shows up," Holly said.

"Something about the cloud of sand and debris brings him running," I said.

"Let's make a cloud then," said Tommy.

I reeled in the line while Tommy uncoiled a section of hose. He fired up the generator and we all watched the pressure inside the compressor's air tank increase. He nodded when he was ready. Holly went over the side. I handed her the hose.

"Just kick some dust up and get out of there," I told her.

Tommy, Shirley, and I leaned over the side, trying to follow Holly's movements. The compressor kicked in when she opened the valve. Within seconds the water was roiled up with blown sand and mud. The debris bloomed up towards us like a mushroom cloud. I started pulling the hose back up. Holly came up with it. Tommy and I grabbed her and pulled her into the boat.

Sure enough, Mr. Hammerhead showed up on cue to investigate. I quickly impaled another piece of beef and spooled it out behind the boat. I hung it there, just on the edge of the cloud. The big shark went right to it. My knuckles were white on the rod. Slam! The beef disappeared within the maul of the shark. He rocketed away from the boat. Line peeled off the rod at an alarming pace. It was like he didn't even know he was hooked.

I moved the drag lever to the strike position. When the line came tight, I slammed the hook home several times. That woke him up. He thrashed his head back and forth a dozen times, turned left, and dug down deep. I eased the drag a little tighter.

"Don't tighten her up too much," yelled Tommy.

"Don't let him spool you," yelled Holly.

"Whoop that sum bitch," yelled Shirley.

My arms started to burn. My lower back started to complain. When the shark slowed, I tried to pull back on him. That's when I heard the pop from my rib cage. I almost lost the rod when the pain shot through my side. Holly was on it. She grabbed the rod and fought the shark standing up. Shirl and Tommy removed the harness from my now worthless body and put it on Holly. She worked her way into the chair. I slumped down in the corner and watched Tommy and Shirley hold onto Holly and the chair at the same time. That damn shark had busted my rib again. It hadn't healed enough to withstand the strain. I could hardly breathe.

Holly held her own with the beast. He swam back and forth behind the boat, slowly tiring. Each time she got him close, he would reach down deep and fight some more. Line was lost. Line was regained. Holly was covered in sweat. I reached for a towel and threw it to Shirley. She wiped Holly's face and neck.

"My arms are going to snap," cried Holly. "I need help."

Tommy took a turn in the chair. The shark was clearly losing, but his weight alone was enough to make him hard to reel in. What life he had left in him, he used. A few swipes of his tail and he gained fifty feet of line. Eventually, his runs got shorter. Tommy drew him closer and closer to the back of the boat.

"Man the winch control," said Tommy. "Bring that big hook down. Grab the tow rope."

I obeyed his orders. When the hook came within reach, Holly grabbed it. Together we fashioned a noose in one end of the rope. We looped the other end over the hook. Tommy had the shark with a few feet of the boat.

"Bring him around to the port side," I said.

"I can't move him," he screamed. "Holly. Help."

She went to his side. He gave her a look of desperation. He'd had enough. She took the rod and walked towards the port gunnel. She couldn't weigh more than a hundred and ten, but she slowly dragged that thousand pound fish to the side of the boat.

"Get his tail quick," she yelled. "I can't hold him for long."

Tommy and I brought the outrigger around until the hook and tow rope hung over the big fish. Holly was groaning in pain while we fiddled with the rope. Each time I thought I had his tail lassoed, he'd swish it out of the way. It was like he knew what we were trying to do. Shirley appeared with a boat hook. She used it to guide the loop into position.

"Now!" she screamed.

I yanked the rope, closing the noose. We had him.

"Up!" I yelled.

Tommy started winding the winch back up. Holly dropped the rod on the deck and laid out on her back.

"Start the pumps," said Tommy. "Get the water flowing."

I flipped the switches and seawater filled the hold. Up came the shark. He watched us with his big shark eyes. His gills moved in a fruitless effort to breathe. Tommy and I turned him and positioned him over the open hatch.

"Down," said Tommy.

Shirley ran to lower the winch. She'd proven herself worthy that day. That tough old bird still had some life left in her. The shark was lowered into the hold. We put enough slack in the rope to allow him some tail movement. He held himself into the stream of incoming water and filled his gills with oxygen. We had him, and he was still alive.

I took a look around. Except for Shirley, my motley crew was broken. It felt like I had a knife in my side. Tommy sat motionless in the deck chair, rubbing his arms. Holly hadn't gotten up from the deck. The rod lay beside her, still attached to the shark. I went to her. After cutting the heavy line, I kneeled beside her.

"You were awesome," I said. "Great job."

"No more shark fishing for me," she said. "Fuck that."

"I thought we were going to have to put Shirley on the rod for a while," I said. "But you beat him."

"He beat me too," she said. "No way I'm diving today."

"Me neither," said Tommy.

"Well ain't this a kick in the pants," said Shirley. "The gold is just sitting down there. You all gonna let a stupid fish keep you from it?"

"I don't know if he'll live through the night," I said. "Let's just rest for a bit. One of us will come around."

I doubted it would be me. I couldn't move my arm without sending shooting pains down my side. I still had trouble breathing. My money was on Holly. She was young and tough as nails. Tommy looked ready for a nap. We should have been celebrating, but everyone was too tired to move. I went to the cooler and brought back four beers. The sound of a pop top snapped Tommy awake. I helped Holly prop herself up and handed her one, knowing that she'd been on the wagon for months. She took it. When everyone had a beer in their hand, I made a toast.

"Here's to big sharks and gold bars," I said, raising my beer up high.

The toast was returned, but with little enthusiasm.

Tommy and I drank more beer. Shirley paced. Holly slowly pulled herself together, refusing another beer. We sat around recalling the battle. Each of us had played a part. It was a shared victory. At the end of retelling the tale, I reenacted Holly falling out on the deck. She laughed. The mood was lightened. The blood was pumping again.

"I'm ready," said Holly. "Let's do this thing."

She sat in the chair while Shirley and I collected her dive gear. Tommy unhooked the winch cable from the tow rope. He used a thick dock line to secure it, so it wouldn't fall in with the shark. He attached the mesh basket.

Holly listened as Tommy explained the attachments and valve use.

"Start by slightly cracking it open," he said. "If you need more juice, open it up a little more. Be conservative. If you open it all the way, it'll flip you around like a rag doll. Don't ask me how I know."

We all laughed at the mental picture of Tommy flapping around like a rag doll underwater.

"Okay, I got it," said Holly. "I'm ready."

She went over the side. Shirley fed out her air hose. I unwound the pressure hose. Tommy lowered the basket. We had a shark in the hold and a diver on the gold.

Fifteen

The compressor kicked in. Sand started to fly. Holly had to pause occasionally due to poor visibility. As soon as the cloud dispersed, she was back at it. She had the heavy marker to work around. She knew just where to clear the sand. A full hour passed before she surfaced. We helped her aboard.

"It's all cleared," she said. "I just need a break."

"You want one of us to load the basket?" I asked.

"Bullshit," she said. "I did all the work. I get the glory."

"You deserve it," I said. "Take it easy."

She drank a bottle of water and caught her breath. Shirley bugged her about the gold. The shark banged the side of the hold. Tommy was working on his sixth beer. I swallowed some more Advil.

Holly went back under about an hour before sunset. It had been a very long day. I couldn't see her down there, but I pictured her loading the basket with gold bars and little gold men. It didn't take her long. She came up and told us she was done. Tommy raised the basket. Shirley went over and peered over the side as the winch brought up our prize. The sun hit the gold and bounced off Shirley's face, giving her a golden glow. Her mouth was open. She had both hands on her face. She had tears in her eyes. Holly smiled. I smiled. Tommy smiled.

Shirley grabbed her chest and stepped back from the rail. She gave me a look of horror. She pointed at her heart. She dropped into the deck chair and gasped for breath.

"Good lord," she panted. "Don't let me die now."

"She's having a heart attack," said Tommy.

"Give her oxygen," said Holly.

"Relax Shirley," I said. "You're going to be okay. Hang in there old girl."

"My ticker," she said.

"Don't talk," I said. "Lay back and breathe."

We used Holly's dive tank to give her air. When she spit it out, Holly stuck it back in her mouth. She calmed. She started getting good deep breaths. She kept a hand over her heart.

"She needs a hospital," said Holly.

"We'll have to call for help," I said. "It will take us hours to get there. The closest one is Port Charlotte, or maybe Cape Coral."

"Do I just dial 911?" she asked.

"Yea," I answered. "There's a rescue boat in Boca Grande. It can be here in minutes."

"We need to hide the gold before they get here," said Tommy.

We'd all forgotten about the gold. It was in piles on the deck, still inside the basket. Roughly forty gold bars and three statues still reflected the setting sun. Shirley stared at it. She'd spent a lifetime to get to this moment. Now she was fighting for her life. It didn't seem fair.

Tommy and I worked to stow our loot inside the cabin. I'd have to hide in there with it when help arrived. I didn't want to be seen by anyone even vaguely connected to law enforcement. Tommy went out to put the outrigger back in place and tidy things up. Holly called for help. The fire/rescue boat arrived in ten minutes. They put Shirley on a backboard and hooked her up to oxygen. A chopper was on its way to the dock.

"Where will they take her?" asked Holly.

"Port Charlotte," the paramedic replied. "You can come with us, but they won't let you in the chopper."

"I'll get there on my own," she said. "We'll have to secure her boat. We'll check on her tomorrow."

They took off at a high rate of speed towards Boca Grande. For the second time in a day, a celebration had to be suspended. Instead of dancing and cheering our riches, we sat in silent sadness. Darkness fell. Tommy went to bed. I sat in the chair, sipping from a bottle of rum.

"I can take her boat up the harbor," said Holly. "Grab a cab. Go check on her."

"I'd go," I said. "But it would be a real risk."

"Stay here," she said. "Get both boats anchored up safe inside the bay. I'll find out how she's doing and come right back."

"Thanks, Holly," I said. "You're the best."

"I can see why you and her are friends," she said. "The old girl kinda grows on you."

"Man, I hope she makes it," I said. "She's rich now."

"Us too," said Holly. "As soon as we sell the stuff anyway."

"We did good work today," I said. "Especially you. I just wish we could enjoy the moment."

"We'll have a big party after we cash in," she said. "Shirley will be the guest of honor."

The shark thumped in the hold below us.

"Shit," I said. "How do you forget you've got a ten-foot hammerhead on board?"

"One of those days, I guess," said Holly.

"We've got to get him back in the water," I said.

We shook off our fatigue and sprang into action. The outrigger boom was turned around to sit over the hold opening. The winch lowered the big hook down to where we could reach it. I pulled the dock line that Tommy had tied off to the tow rope until I could grab it. I tugged on the rope. The shark tugged back. He was still kicking. I hooked the tow rope and Holly raised the winch. Up came the shark. His big shark eyes looked at us again. He'd have a story to tell his buddies tomorrow.

We used boat hooks to swing him over the gunnel and suspend him over the water. We had to get the rope off of his tail somehow. This presented a problem. We looked at each other.

"How's this going to work?" asked Holly.

"We've got to lower him enough so that we can reach the loop," I said.

"He'll be in the water by then," she said. "And pissed off."

"Bring him down some," I said.

Holly lowered the shark until his head was in the water. He thrashed about violently. He was so close to escaping, but still unable to swim.

"Get me your dive knife," I said.

She handed me the knife. I reached out over the rail and slid the knife between the shark's tail and the rope. Thank God for sharp knives. The rope parted. The shark slid down the side of the boat into the sea. He hovered there for a second, then swam off slowly like nothing had happened at all. He was free. Holly and I exchanged high-fives.

"Seems like a good time to remind you of something," said Holly. "This mission was supposed to be a walk in the park. No danger."

"Shit happens," I said. "Let's go. I'm beat."

We took the dinghy back to *Freedom*. We were both too tired to consider sex. We went straight to our respective bunks. I took a minute to wish Shirley well, before falling asleep. I slept like a rock. The sun had long been up when I awoke. Holly wasn't in her bunk. She wasn't even on board. I stuck my head out the back door. Shirley's little sailboat was coming towards me. Holly waved from behind the wheel.

"I should be back before dark," she said. "Go anchor inside the bay."

I turned on the coffee maker and hailed Tommy on the radio.

"Good morning, sunshine," he said. "Hell of a day yesterday."

"Follow me in," I said. "Thirty minutes or so. Then we can relax for the day."

"Sounds like a plan," he said. "I'll follow you."

I drank my coffee and took some more Advil. The rib was thumping. At least I had a day to rest. I hoped Holly would return with good news. I hoped Tommy wouldn't decide to take off without us. He had the gold on his boat, and he was faster than I was. I hadn't thought of that possibility. I didn't know if he was capable of that sort of treachery. It would be a simple thing for him to do.

I needed to clear my head. The pain and the excitement were causing me to miss little details, like a ten-foot shark in the hold, and leaving the gold unattended with Tommy. I fired up the engine, raised the anchor and idled towards the entrance to Pelican Bay. I kept an eye on Tommy's boat. He followed me. Relieved, I throttled up and carried on. Tommy stayed behind me. We both got our anchors down towards the southern part of the bay. The day was clear. There were no signs of foul weather. It was just another sunny day in paradise.

Tommy and I ate breakfast on the rusty shrimper. We talked about what we'd recovered.

"What do you think of those little statues?" I asked him.

"Not my area of expertise," he said. "You'll have to find an antiquities expert."

"You know any?"

"Not a reputable one," he said.

"Black market?" I asked.

"All that shit is black market," he said. "You can't sell it legally. Florida thinks it belongs to them. Spain probably thinks it belongs to them. Some damn insurance company probably thinks it's theirs."

"What's your advice?" I asked him.

"Sell it all for its gold value," he said. "You've probably got a half million there. Clean and easy."

"Not exactly the haul I was hoping for, though," I said.

"Not chump change either," he replied. "Pretty good for a day's work."

"I want to appraise the little gold men before I make up my mind," I said. "And consult with the women."

"Your call," he said. "I hope the old broad is okay."

"Thanks," I said. "Me too."

I went back to my boat and lazed the day away. The quiet was nice. The uncertainty about Shirley's condition was not. This was her find after all. If she died, it would ruin everything. We dug it up for her. Our cut was incidental. Hell, she could have my share if she wanted it. I was worried about her.

My worries were unfounded. An hour before sunset I saw the little sailboat enter the bay. When it got close, I saw Shirley's blonde and gray pigtails sticking out from under her floppy hat. She smiled and waved. Holly was all smiles too. Shirl looked fine. They came over after Holly got them anchored.

"You look fit as a fiddle," I told Shirley. "When you left here you didn't look so hot."

"Pacemaker malfunction," she said. "This damn thing is gonna kill me yet."

"Sensor induced tachycardia," said Holly.

"Say who?"

"The doctor said that all the excitement caused the sensor to misfire," she said. "He used some kind of magnet to reset it."

"I got my own heart rate up faster than the pacemaker can go," said Shirley. "The damn thing got stuck."

"I'm happy they got you fixed up," I said.

"She needs to see her cardiologist," said Holly.

"I'm fine," said Shirley. "And I'm rich."

"Can we celebrate now?" I asked.

Holly and Shirley spoke at the same time.

"Hell yes," they said.

We moved the party over to Tommy's boat. He had pumped the water out of the hold. The old shrimper rode much higher in the water. Holly climbed up first. I helped Shirley out of the dinghy and handed her up to Holly. Tommy acted genuinely happy that Shirley was okay. He passed out beers to all of us.

"Some team we are," he said. "Broken ribs and heart attacks."

"We finished what we came here to do," I said.

"That we did," he said. "Congratulations to all three of you. Well done."

"How much do you think its worth?" Shirley asked.

"Tommy says half a million in gold value alone," I answered.

"I thought we were talking millions," she said.

"That's if the little statues mean something to somebody," I explained. "We'll have to track down the right people."

I brought out the four idols. We passed them around. Holly used her phone to search for similar items. Outside of museums, there wasn't much available. There was one small idol for sale on eBay. The seller claimed it was an Aztec piece. The current high bid was seventy-eight thousand dollars. We couldn't sell ours on eBay. The powers that be would be all over us in a heartbeat. That was it, one piece, not really similar to what we had, on all of the internet.

"These deals go down in dark alleys," Tommy said. "Not on the internet."

"That's what I'm afraid of," I said. "Maybe you're right about taking the gold value."

I turned to the girls.

"What do you think?" I asked them.

"I'm okay with it," said Holly.

"Can't we find out what these are worth first?" said Shirley.

"We can try," I said. "If you're not in a hurry."

"I guess I should be in a hurry," she said. "With this ticker."

"We'll give a quick shot," I said. "I'll talk to the Mel Fisher woman. If it's going to be a huge hassle, or in any way dangerous, we'll give it up."

"It's going to be dangerous," Tommy said. "No way around it."

Holly cleared her throat loudly. The word *dangerous* was being thrown around too often for her liking. I couldn't blame her. I wrapped the idols up in a cloth and put them away.

"One shot," I said.

"One shot," said Shirley.

Tommy shrugged.

"Okay, damn it," Holly said. "One quick shot."

We convinced Shirley to make an appointment with her cardiologist. There was no need for her to tag along with us to Key West. We'd turn the gold into cash, one way or another. We'd bring her share back to her. Once she was finished with the doctor, she'd go back to Goodland and wait. Holly was anxious to get back to her boat. Tommy was anxious to recover his gold. We all pulled up and left the bay the next morning.

Sixteen

Holly took a bunch of pictures of the gold bars and the little gold men with her phone. It made me reconsider owning one. She used it all the time to check the weather, calculate math problems, and search Google for answers. It would certainly come in handy, but I was paranoid about the feds tracking me somehow. It was best to go on living without a phone. It gave me a strange peace of mind. I couldn't be bothered if I had no phone.

Holly and I went to Boot Key Harbor. Tommy went back to Key Largo. *Another Adventure* was safe and secure on a mooring ball. I anchored in the creek, away from most of the prying eyes. We arranged another meeting at the Mel Fisher Museum. I carried the four idols in a backpack. The bus ride took an hour. The director was waiting for us when we arrived.

"They don't look Aztec," she said. "Or Incan, or Mayan, or like anything else I've ever seen."

"What else could they be?" I asked. "And who would know?"

"This is an extremely specialized field," she said. "There's only a handful of people on earth that could determine their origin."

"Where do I find one of these people?"

"Costa Rica," she said.

"You've got to be kidding me," I said.

"There's a Pre-Columbian Gold Museum in San Jose," she said. "They've got figurines and statues like these. They are the world's authority on the Pre-Columbian period."

"We can't go to Costa Rica," Holly said.

"Why not?" I asked. "You've got a sailboat."

"One quick shot, you said."

"One quick shot down to Costa Rica," I said. "It'll be fun."

"Let me make a phone call," the director said. "I'll let them know to expect you."

She left the room.

"Christ, Breeze," Holly said. "Costa Freaking Rica?"

"Think of it as a vacation," I said. "The FBI won't be a problem. We can both relax."

"What about Tommy?" she asked.

"Call him," I said. "Tell him we'll be back in two weeks or so."

"He's not going to be happy," she said.

"I'll talk to him," I said. "I'll promise we'll be there to help him. We won't let him down."

On the bus ride back to Marathon, Holly came around. She agreed, sailing for a week would be fun. She loved nothing more. She was in. I put her in charge of provisioning for the trip. I stuck my nose in the charts to see what we were getting ourselves into. I called Tommy. He admitted that he was pretty tired. The rest would do him good. His gold could wait another few weeks. Planning a trip to a new destination was exciting. I hadn't been past Grand Cayman in that part of the world. That's where I'd first met Holly.

Problems with the plan started to pop up. San Jose was far inland, not near the coast. The biggest river had a dam across it. The smaller river was too small for Holly's boat. Costa Rica was a long way from Marathon. I couldn't use my passport for fear of the FBI being alerted. This was turning out to be a dumb idea. I couldn't fly due to the passport issue. I couldn't fly with a bunch of gold in my possession either. We'd have to find a safe place to anchor. We'd have to find transportation over land to the museum, in a foreign country. Holly was going to hate it.

I decided to omit some of the details. She'd be happy to sail. Once we were there, she'd have no choice but to go along. It wasn't the smartest choice I'd ever made, but I was up against a wall. One quick shot was looking like an ordeal. *Way to go, Breeze.*

I turned on my chart plotter to get a feel for the trip. If we traveled a straight line from Marathon to the coast of Costa Rica, we'd cover just over one thousand miles. Sailboats don't normally travel in straight lines. With the proper winds and little tacking, we'd travel at least eleven hundred miles. It would take a week to get there if things went well. The weather forecast was favorable. Solid east winds would push us along at seven or eight knots. There were no hurricanes or major storms on the horizon.

I stashed *Freedom* at the Marathon Boat Yard. I could trust Howie to keep an eye on it. Holly had filled her boat with food, fuel, and water. *Another Adventure* was ready for another adventure. We left at dawn on a cool autumn day. We aimed our bow to the southwest. After clearing Cuban waters, we'd veer south towards Central America. Holly fiddled with the trim of the sails until she was happy. We sliced through a light chop in the Florida Straits at a brisk eight knots.

We spent our days trolling a lure behind us. We alternated shifts at night. We ate fresh fish and breathed in the salt air. I avoided alcohol, wanting to be on the top of my game in case of trouble. The wind remained in our favor. We made excellent time. Day after day, night after night, we pushed on. I'd gradually become a better sailor, thanks to Holly's tutelage. We became better as a team too. Not just any couple can sail across the open ocean for a week straight, without driving each other batty. We got along with each other fine. We got along with the boat and the sea. I was almost sorry to see the trip end. We had no worries out there. It was land that caused the worry. Land meant people. People meant trouble.

We were able to navigate a mile or so into the Reventazon River. We poked around until we found a small cove out of the current. We anchored behind some rocks for better protection. There were no signs of civilization. As we sat and took a look around, I heard a truck in the distance. There was a road. Occasionally, I heard a car go by. The road was through some thick foliage and up a mid-sized rise. We hiked up the hill the next morning. It was not easy going. Our deck shoes didn't make for good climbing footwear. A machete to clear our path would have been nice. The bugs were big and mean. My side started to ache before we reached the top, but the noise of the cars grew louder.

When we finally emerged from the jungle to find the road, we were exhausted and sweaty. A truck roared by before we could flag him down. The road ran inland, paralleling the river. After a short rest, we started walking. There wasn't much traffic. Three cars passed us by before someone stopped. A creaky old Suzuki pulled off to the side. We ran up to it.

"San Jose, por favor," I said, waving a twenty dollar bill.

"Si, San Jose," the driver said.

That was the end of our conversation. No one spoke during the entire ride until we made the city center.

"Museum de Oro," I said, in my best Spanglish."

The old man behind the wheel seemed to understand. Sure enough, a few minutes later we stopped in front of the Pre-Columbian Gold Museum.

"Gracias, senor," I said.

He said nothing as we exited the old car.

"Well, you did it again," Holly said. "Off on a wing and a prayer and here we are."

"Piece of cake," I said. "You worry too much."

"Life's a Breeze," she said. "I can't imagine why I'd think that somehow this would go wrong for us. It's not like you have a track record or anything."

"Shit works out," I said.

"I know, I know," she said. "Let's go find out about these little gold men."

The meeting with the museum curator did not go as planned. He was a fastidious little man who spoke excellent English. Behind his desk, the shelves were lined with textbooks and photo albums. He assured us that we'd come to the right place. As far as he knew, there was no one else on Earth who possessed his experience working with Pre-Colombian gold. That's why we were surprised when he couldn't identify the pieces we'd brought to him.

"Not Aztec," he said. "Not even from the same period. I am certain that these are not authentic."

"What do you mean, not authentic?" I asked.

"They match no known example of anything ever found in Central or even South America," he said.

"What can that mean?" I asked. "Where did they come from?"

"Someone made them, obviously," he said. "Much more modern techniques."

"You mean modern day?" I asked. "They're fakes?"

"Probably not recent," he said. "Maybe early nineteenth century, possibly newer."

"I don't know what to think about this," I admitted. "Curious."

"How did you come into possession of these pieces?" he asked. "If you don't mind my asking. I'm curious too."

"We pulled them up from the ocean floor," I told him.

"Florida?"

"Boca Grande Pass," I said. "Nearer to Cayo Costa."

"I am familiar with this island," he said. "There was once a small settlement there. It died off in the early nineteen hundreds. Many tales of Gasparilla."

"They were fishermen and boat builders," I said. "Not gold traders."

"If you will humor me," he said. "We have a study on the Gulf coast barrier islands. No significant gold find has ever been discovered in the area."

He left the room for several minutes, leaving us to stand around and twiddle our thumbs. We looked at each other and shrugged. He returned with a file box containing maps, charts, and research writings. He pulled out an overview of the Boca Grande Pass, showing both Gasparilla Island and Cayo Costa.

"Right here," I said, pointing to the spot where we found the gold.

"If it was underwater," he began. "It had to come from a ship or smaller boat."

"Lots of boats have gone down on Johnson Shoals over the years," I said. "But that's out there. The gold would sink and be on the shoals, not where we found it."

"Maybe the boat holed on the reef, but continued inshore before finally going down?"

"Possibility," I said. "No signs of wreckage. No cannons, or pottery or the like."

"Could a wooden chest float for a while before sinking?" asked Holly. "Then it rotted away over the years. The bars were all lined up in a neat row."

"Anything is possible at this point," I said.

"What other distinguishing characteristics did the target area have?" asked the curator.

"Ballast stones," I said. "Ships anchored there for quarantine. They'd lighten their load before going up Charlotte Harbor to Punta Gorda."

"So the gold could have come from an anchored vessel," he said. "Tossed overboard for some reason."

"Still doesn't explain the figurines," I said.

"I think you may have had a real pirate on Cayo Costa after all," he said. "The gold was melted down into bars, but someone on one of those boats learned to make his own figures. A pirate sculptor if you may."

"Crazy theory," I said. "Pirates steal gold figures, then melt them down into bars. One guy decided to use the melted gold to pour new statues. The whole lot ends up overboard. I don't know."

"We will probably never know," he said. "And I have more bad news for you."

"Great," said Holly. "What now?"

"The gold is not particularly pure," he said. "It's contaminated with copper. The original idols must have been adorned with copper. It all got melted down together. A metallurgist could separate them, but it would be more expense than it's worth."

"So the gold did originally come from ancient times?" I asked.

"All gold comes from ancient times," he said. "The original idols would be valuable to collectors, but what you have is not authentic. I caution you not to attempt to pass them off as legitimate."

"So all we have is a pile of impure gold," I said. "Not what we'd hoped to learn."

"I am sorry, Mr. Breeze," he said. "You've come a long way to be disappointed."

"Not your fault," I said. "I appreciate your expertise."

"I would suggest a reputable wholesaler," he said. "All is not lost."

"Thanks."

We left the museum with our tails between our legs. We were not going to be fantastically rich. Shirley wouldn't be leaving millions to her daughter. We still had a long way to go to get back to Florida. First, we had to get back to the boat.

"Let's go to Costa Rica, he said. It will be fun, he said," said Holly. "Shit works out, he said."

"Hey, we had to take a shot," I said.

"It wasn't a quick one," she said. "Nor was it profitable."

"I'm sorry," I said. "But it's not like we had anything better to do."

"It was a good sail," she admitted. "I hope it will be as good going home."

"Your phone doesn't work down here, does it?" I asked.

"No, it doesn't," she said. "We should have looked into a SIM card before we left."

"I'm not sure there's much infrastructure for the internet here," I said. "At least not away from the city."

"So we've got no weather information," she said.

"That's right."

"Should we try a café or something?" she asked. "Somebody's got to have Wi-Fi."

San Jose was a modern city. It even had a McDonald's. Sure enough, the McDonald's had free Wi-Fi, just like in the U.S. Holly studied the weather for a long time.

"There's a potential thing," she said.

"A thing?"

"Yea, five days out," she said. "A wave or something."

"Tropical wave?" I asked. "Not good."

"It's just a possibility right now," she said. "Gonna be windy, though."

"How windy?"

"Twenty to thirty," she said. "Still doable."

"You're the captain," I said.

"Let's get out of here," she said. "Let's go home."

We thumbed a ride back to the boat. Having Holly along made hitching much easier. Who wouldn't pick up a pretty young rasta chick? We hacked and snaked our way back down the hill to the dinghy. It was untouched. I doubt anyone even knew it was there. Back on *Another Adventure,* fatigue set in. Both of us suffered from long days at sea followed by long hikes up and down that damned hill. I went straight to bed and slept for ten hours.

When I woke up, Holly had her vessel ready to sail. She handed me a cup of coffee and moved forward to pull up the anchor.

"You in a hurry to sail into a storm?" I asked.

"You snuck us into a foreign country a thousand miles from home," she said. "I just want to get out of here."

"I'd like to suggest a slight detour," I said.

"Where?" she asked. "And why?"

"Grand Cayman," I answered. "We can recheck the weather from there. Maybe I can catch up with my friend Theo."

"It will add a couple days to the trip," she said.

"It will break it up," I said. "Give us both a break."

"Okay," she said. "Makes sense. Plot us a course."

We sailed away from the coast and out into the open ocean. We'd had no trouble with any kind of authorities in Costa Rica. We'd had no luck getting rich off of our gold either. It was depressing really. We'd been through a lot to get that pile of crude bars. We'd all had dreams of becoming filthy rich. After splitting it with Shirley, then halving what was left, Holly and I wouldn't gain very much. I'd been paying all the expenses. I'd cover that with a little left over. We still had to find someone to buy it. We still had to help Tommy recover his riches.

I could sense that Holly was less than thrilled with the outcome of this little adventure. There were only so many times I could say *what else do you have to do?* She'd wanted tangible results, not just stories to tell. I'd been on other missions that didn't result in financial benefit. The money meant little to me, as long as I could survive and have a cold beer now and then. Finishing the job was reward enough. Having an objective, executing a plan, reaching your goal; those things were what drove me.

I wasn't sure what Holly's motives were. She'd longed for freedom on the high seas when I first met her. She'd had her shot at it. The dream grew old and she'd returned to Florida. What was she seeking in Florida? Was it a relationship? Was it a career? She seemed to bounce back and forth between a thirst for adventure and a need for some sense of normalcy. She'd once decided that I wasn't a part of her future, but she jumped at the chance to pair back up with me when offered. I'd tried to leave her memory behind in the Dominican, but it never fully left me. The line between friend and lover was seriously blurred for us. We made a great team, until the time came to make any final decisions about a future together.

We sailed on. *Another Adventure* sliced the waves of the Caribbean Sea on our way northward. The wind was right. The sails were trimmed to perfection. We made good time. During my night watch on the fourth night, I had to wake Holly. I could see lightning in the distance. It was time to alter course and steer for Grand Cayman. The winds had freshened out of the east.

"We're going to have to beat into it," Holly said. "We'll lose speed and it will get rough."

"The storm is probably over Cuba," I said.

"All that matters is the wind and the waves," she countered. "Run us northeast for a mile or two, then tack back southeast."

"Got it," I said. "We'll zig zag into it."

"Keep a close reach," she instructed. "I'll reef the main."

We fought our way for hours until it seemed we weren't moving at all. As much as Holly hated it, we decided to fire the engine. I took the wheel as she brought down the main. We left a little bit of jib out. As I shifted into forward, the gears ground badly.

"What the hell was that?" she yelled.

"Transmission isn't happy," I said. "You change the oil in it lately?"

"Not in forever," she admitted.

"Do you have any transmission fluid?" I asked.

"I've got ninety weight," she said.

"Gear oil?" I asked. "Tranny fluid is light, not thick."

"Shit, I don't know," she said. "I'm not prepared for this."

I motioned for her to take the wheel. I couldn't help but think that I had a case of transmission fluid onboard my boat. I went below and lifted the hatch to the engine room. The transmission was making a nasty noise. I touched the housing. It was hot. I pulled the dipstick. Nothing but a gummy stain showed on it. We needed to put fluid in it, now. I went back up and shut down the engine.

"We'll burn your tranny up in minutes," I said. "But I don't think gear oil is the answer."

"Thirty weight?" she asked, sheepishly.

"Still too thick," I said. "But what choice do we have?"

"Sails up and slamming for another day," she said. "We tack back and forth out here and hope the storm doesn't come this way."

"That doesn't have much appeal for me," I said. "But it's your boat. If we motor, we'll likely kill the transmission."

"Can we fix it in Grand Cayman?" she asked.

"Most likely," I said. "Won't be cheap."

"Fantastic," she said. "This trip just keeps getting better and better."

"We'll take it out of my share," I said.

"If we ever get any shares at all," she said. "Who goes hunting for junk gold? Fighting frigging sharks. Crossing oceans. Jesus, Breeze, this thing has been a nightmare and it's never going to pay off. I should have just stayed in the Keys, cleaning boat bottoms. Safer that way."

"You would have missed all the fun," I said. "You wouldn't have met Shirl and Tommy.

You wouldn't have wrestled a monster hammerhead. You wouldn't have seen Shirley's face when that basket of gold came up."

"That was pretty sweet," she said. "Until she had a damn heart attack."

"Bumps in the road, baby," I said. "Make the best of what life throws at you. Now, what do you want to do?"

"Fuck it," she said. "Fire the motor back up. Run her till she blows."

Seventeen

The transmission almost got us into port. We lost forward gear just after passing through the outer reef. It gave out a high-pitched whine before letting go. The engine revved dangerously high as a result. Holly was quick to throttle back. She wiggled the shifter. Reverse still worked.

"Drop the jib," she yelled. "I'll back us in."

I ran forward to pull down the last remaining bit of sail. Holly jammed the transmission into reverse and we spun around. We backed through the harbor until we got close enough to shore to drop anchor safely. Smoke poured out of the engine room. The tranny was toast.

The radio crackled. Harbor patrol wanted to know if we needed a fire boat. A local offered to tow us into the marina for a hundred bucks. We politely declined both.

"Well, here we are," said Holly. "Halfway home in a broken boat. Got any more brilliant ideas?"

"We'll go into town and see if someone can help us," I said. "Get a weather update. Worse thing we could do is sail her on back to the Keys."

"I'm thinking a certain salty son of a bitch owes a girl a nice dinner out," she said.

"It's the least a salty son of a bitch could do," I said. "We have enough water for showers?"

"Maybe we should share a shower," she suggested. "Just to make sure we don't run out."

"Excellent idea," I said. "We'll both be less salty sons of bitches."

The playful romp under hot running water improved our moods. We'd had a tough two weeks, but life was still good. We were playing out on Mother Ocean. It was what we both loved the most about life. I put on my best shirt. Holly wore her least wrinkled outfit. We took the dinghy into the yacht club and shared a nice meal. We forgot about life for a while.

After our meal, we walked the waterfront, hand in hand. It wasn't like us to share tender moments like that. We'd been on the go for two years, chasing bad guys and chasing gold. We paused occasionally for sex of varying degrees of passion. We enjoyed watching the sunsets, but we never just held each other's hand. It was sweet. Maybe there was hope for us when the mission was over.

The magic was somewhat broken when we got drenched on the dinghy ride back to her boat. Taking off our wet clothes seemed like a perfect excuse to share a bunk, but it wasn't to be. Holly gave me a gentle stiff arm and said good night. I sat naked and alone out in the cockpit, contemplating the meaning of life.

I needed to turn the mission around. The impure gold needed to be sold for as much as we could get for it. I'd fix up Shirley. Holly would have a little financial independence. We still had to deal with Tommy and his own treasure. Then what? I couldn't predict what would happen next. I took one long slug of rum and called it a night.

I dreamt the same scene over and over again in a recurring loop. Holly's sails disappeared over the horizon. It was the same scene I'd witnessed when we parted ways in the Dominican. White sails, blue seas, and a lonely heart. I'd had a chance in that moment to change my future. I could have gone back to Luperon and into the arms of a different lovely woman. I could have lived out my days with her in a tropical paradise. I'd have never seen Holly again. There was still a twinge of loss for that woman, but I was glad to be right where I was. Holly was just a few feet away, breathing softly and dreaming her own dreams. If I only knew what they were.

The morning broke gray and windy. We suffered through another wet ride on our way into town. We stopped by the yacht club again to take advantage of the Wi-Fi.

"This system should clear out of here tonight," said Holly. "After that, we're looking at light west winds."

"Enough to make us go?" I asked.

"Ten knots or less," she said. "We'll be crawling but it will move us."

"Should we try to get it fixed or replaced here?" I asked.

"We've got a nice little window starting tomorrow," she said. "I say we take it and run. There's no sign of trouble in the five-day forecast."

"Probably cheaper in Florida anyway," I said. "I'm game if you are."

"We sail tomorrow," she announced. "You want to look up your friend?"

All it took was a visit to the dock master. I asked him to call us a cab, specifying Theo. My old pal pulled up in minutes. No dope smoke rolled out when he opened the door. He was sharply dressed and well groomed. I almost didn't recognize him. The assorted baubles and ornaments were gone from his dreadlocks. He wore nice shoes instead of sandals. He looked professional.

"That you, Breeze?" he said. "I didn't think I'd ever see you again."

"You're looking good, man," I said. "Turned over a new leaf?"

"First I quit the booze," he said. "And then I quit the leaf. I make my wife very happy."

"You look happy too," I said. "And I'm happy for you."

"What brings you back to our island?"

"Passing through. Lost a transmission," I said. "You happen to know where I can get a new one?"

"For your boat?" he asked.

"Sailboat," I said.

"No man," he said. "You can get one for them big Caterpillars or Detroits down here. But this is not sailboat country."

"I didn't think so," I said. "Thanks anyway. You got time for lunch?"

"I really shouldn't," he said. "I'm a business-man now. Got three cabs."

"That's great, Theo," I said.

"It all started to turn around when you were here the first time," he said. "That money you gave me, it got me on my feet. I can't thank you enough."

"It was your doing," I said. "But I'm happy to have helped."

"I do have one curious piece of information for you," he said. "The man you came here to find."

"Jimi Dinapoli?" I asked.

"He was here," he said. "I saw him one day, then nothing. I asked around like you did. I was curious. No one saw him again."

"Jimi D. was here?" asked Holly. "What would he be doing here?"

"Probably cleaning up some banking business," I guessed. "No telling where he is now."

"He came through for us, Breeze," said Holly. "He took care of me and the boat when we left the Exumas. He stepped up, big time. I just wanted you to know."

"There a glimmer of hope for him yet," I said. "He's not all bad. I wish him well."

"Me too," she said. "Me too."

We said our goodbyes to Theo the business-man. We loaded up some groceries and took them back out to *Another Adventure*. We anticipated smooth, if not slow sailing on the last leg back to Florida.

At first, I wasn't sure we were moving at all. Holly had every thread of sail up, but none of it filled with any wind. There was no current to speak of. Eventually, I could detect a slight

forward motion. We limped along impercep-
tibly, sails sagging. It took hours for us to
clear the northernmost point of land. After
that, we picked up a light breeze. The sails
puffed out a bit. *Another Adventure* carried us
towards the northwest at four knots. We set a
course to clear the western shore of Cuba and
settled in.

It was a boring ride. Holly's boat was heavy
and carried a deep draft. She was at her best
in heavy wind. There was barely a ripple on
the sea as the winds varied from zero to five
knots. It was hot. This was one of the reasons
I'd never own a sailboat. The winds were
either too strong, too light, or coming from
the wrong direction. We couldn't fire up the
diesel with no transmission. Florida seemed to
be a million miles away.

After two days of bobbing about, our nerves
began to wear thin. I tried napping but the
heat made it impossible. Holly cast a fishing
rod off the stern. Nothing was interested. We
steered well clear of Cuban waters. Once we
turned towards the northwest, the winds
carried us a little faster. We had a downwind
run to Marathon. Holly adjusted the sails to
her liking, and we settled back in.

"Once we finish helping Tommy," she said. "I think I'm going to bail."

"Seriously?" I asked. "I thought we were getting along just swell."

"It's not that," she said. "It's the bigger picture."

"No future with a boat bum like me?"

"You're a lot more than a boat bum," she said. "And therein lies the problem."

"Not following you," I said.

"Whenever I get hooked up with you," she began. "We get caught up in some crazy adventure. Costa Rica this time. Shooting Taylor in the Bahamas. It's just nuts."

"I didn't plan for any of that to happen," I said.

"You never plan for anything," she said. "Maybe you should. People get caught up in your world, Breeze. Your choices have a profound effect on others, whether you like it or not. It's weird because you try to stay a ghost, but there it is. My life isn't my own when I'm with you. The same can be said for Jimi D. You suck people in and things get out of control for everyone involved."

"I spend so much energy trying to be self-aware," I said. "Maybe I should have been trying to be more aware of my friend's feelings."

"I know you don't mean any harm," she said. "You try to help. Like now, this is all for Shirley, but look what you're putting us through."

"I thought it would be an adventure for us to share," I said. "Plus coming down here kept me off the FBI's radar."

"That's another thing," she said. "They should be looking for me, not you. How do things get so screwed up?"

"Thought I was doing you a favor," I said.

"If we weren't in that situation in the first place," she said. "None of it would have ever happened."

"We can't change what happened," I said. "But I'm sorry if it means anything."

"You're just being you," she said. "It's what you do. It's who you are. I just don't think I can continue to live like this."

"After we cash in," I said. "We can take a long vacation. Forget all about missions."

"I think I need a vacation from you," she said. "I'll finish what we started, but after that, I've got to go my own way. I need to think for myself. Figure shit out on my own."

"Fair enough," I said. "As long as it's not a permanent goodbye."

"We both suck at those," she admitted. "Until we meet again seems more appropriate, but no promises."

The rest of the trip was spent in sullen introspection. I had to admit that I'd been selfish in my pursuits. I just gave orders and expected my friends to follow them. I was the self-appointed leader, but Holly was no follower. She was my equal in so many ways. She was an awesome sailor and diver. She'd been fearless when confronting Taylor. She fought sharks, swam like a fish, and turned wrenches with the best of the mechanics I'd ever seen. I'd come to rely on her, maybe even taken her skills for granted. Our love life was always a mystery, but we couldn't deny our friendship. We made good partners, but I'd overstepped my authority time and time again. She was right to reclaim her sense of self. I couldn't deny her that.

We got a little more wind and picked up speed. Holly seemed anxious to make Marathon. She tweaked and adjusted constantly, trying to get the most out of her vessel. I stayed out of her way. I tried to guess what Tommy had in store for us. How much gold did he have hidden away? How hard would it be to recover? What unknown danger was out there waiting for us? The last thing I wanted was to put Holly in harm's way again.

"I'll do the diving for Tommy's gold," I told her. "If you want."

"Nothing personal," she said. "But I'm a hell of a lot better than you. I'll do it."

"Suit yourself," I said. "But the offer is out there. If you feel the least bit wary, just say so."

"I can handle it."

We finally made it to Boot Key Harbor. I watched with respect as Holly sailed us into the mooring field. I stood on the bow with a boat hook. We were down to one sail, which we dumped as we approached the ball. I snatched up the mooring pennant, ran a line through it, and cleated it off. It pulled tight, stopping our forward motion. If I'd have missed, we would have been powerless to come around for another attempt.

"Good job, Breeze," Holly said.

"We could have started the engine and used reverse," I said.

"My ship, my rules," she said.

"Aye, captain."

Our first order of business was to contact Tommy. Holly called him on her cell. We'd been gone too long for his liking. He'd started to worry we wouldn't show up. I had to wonder why he couldn't just get his gold by himself, but we were committed to helping him. He wanted to get started right away. We needed a few days to recover from our trip, and to re-provision. He reluctantly agreed.

Holly wasn't much for conversation as we went about refueling her boat and topping off the water tanks. She'd looked around for some transmission help with little luck. We'd take my boat up to Key Largo to meet Tommy. That meant filling it with fuel and water and buying, even more, groceries. My offer to cover our expenses was coming back to haunt me. I was spending a fortune keeping everyone in fuel and food. I'd also told Holly I'd pay for her transmission. My generosity was costing me, but it was too late to back out.

Freedom appeared to be undisturbed. I winced at the sight of the name on the transom. I wondered what my status was with the FBI. Surely, they'd given up any active search. Like Holly said, I was a ghost. If I could manage not to get arrested or otherwise come into contact with law enforcement, I'd be good. I was familiar with being a wanted man. This wasn't my first rodeo. I secretly wished that Holly had been a little more grateful for me taking the rap. I'd never mention it though, it was all my fault in the first place. I tried to focus on the task at hand. We'd meet Tommy, hear his plan, and get his gold. After that was done, I'd cash us all out. I'd give Shirley her money and go on about my lonely life. I'd wish Holly the best. The FBI would never find me. I'd disappear into the mangrove jungles, catch fish and drink rum until the day I died.

We left for Key Largo three days later. It was a ten hour run up the inside route to Pumpkin

Key. The anchor went down. The beer followed. I sat and drank while Holly talked to Tommy on the phone. He was ready. We were ready. I just wanted to get it over with. Sleep wouldn't come until half a bottle of rum was downed. Holly said goodnight somewhere around my fourth slug straight from the bottle.

It didn't hurt me in the morning. I was a professional drinker after all. Holly would be doing the hard work anyway. We took the dinghy up the creek to Tommy's dock. He was waiting for us aboard the old shrimper. His engine was running.

"Come aboard," he yelled. "I thought you'd never get here."

"What's the rush?" I asked him. "That money burning a hole in your pocket?"

"I've got some new information," he said. "The feds have been watching me. They know."

"Everybody knows you hid some gold, Tommy," I said. "Why now?"

"I got a call from a sympathetic insider," he said. "They were using Fat Albert to keep an eye on me for a while. Then they started sending boats by here on a regular basis."

"So why are we in a hurry, if they're watching so closely?"

"Because that stupid surveillance blimp is otherwise occupied at the moment," he said. "So's the boats. Some big drug interdiction about to happen."

"What if someone follows us?" Holly asked. "We'll lead them right to the gold."

"That's why I need you two," he said.

"Lay it out for us, Tommy," I said.

"You're going to recover it," he said.

"What are you going to do?" I asked.

"I'm taking this here gold recovery vessel out to the reef," he said. "I'll do some diving, maybe get us some lobsters for dinner."

"So if they follow you, you'll be in the wrong spot, diving for lobster."

"You'll be in the right spot, diving for gold," he said.

"You sure you trust us with this?" I asked.

"I haven't got much choice at this point," he said. "But yea, I think you'll come through. Plus, you need a way to fence the gold."

"Speaking of that," I said. "Our gold doesn't amount to much. The idols are almost worthless. The gold isn't pure in the bars either."

"I didn't like the looks of it when it came up," he said. "But I didn't want to burst anyone's bubble."

"Our problem," I said. "Not yours."

"I'll give it some thought," he said. "I've got a lead on a buyer for my coins."

"That's good news," I said.

"We'll see," he said. "You ready to get this show on the road?"

"Let's do it," said Holly.

"Let's go," I said. "Tell us where we're going."

We went inside to the chart table and Tommy pointed out some markings in Florida Bay. He had the coordinates written down on a sticky note. He would take his boat and run outside to the reef off of Angelfish Creek. We'd wait until he was gone, then slowly meander into Florida Bay to a spot near Oxfoot Bank. It was one of the rare deep holes in Florida Bay, surrounded by shallow water. Tommy pointed to red marker number twelve, just off the old Yacht Channel.

"You know what a trot line is?" he asked.

"Sure do," I said. "Used them for crabs back on the Chesapeake."

"I got a line of boxes on mine," he said. "Each of them with fifty pounds of gold inside."

"That's going to be one heavy line to pull," I said.

"Each box is attached to a cable with a stainless carabiner," he said. "Send her down to release one at a time. Haul them up with a line. Both ends of the trot line are marked with buoys. As you're heading north, the red one will be the port end of the line. A green one is on the starboard end. They're old and got a lot of grass hanging on them."

"How many boxes?" I asked.

"Six."

"Three hundred pounds of gold?" I asked. "What's that worth?"

"I can't get what it's worth," he said. "But I can get millions."

"I swear to God," Holly said. "I'm going to dive, but I'm not playing with any guns or bad guys afterward."

"Leave that to me," I said. "I've got to earn my keep somehow."

"We'll talk about after you get the gold," said Tommy. "We got nothing until it's recovered."

"We'll get it," Holly said. "Piece of cake."

"Everybody ready?" I asked.

Tommy and Holly nodded in agreement. We were all ready.

"Today's the day," Tommy said, quoting Mel Fisher.

Eighteen

We watched Tommy take his rusty shrimper into Angelfish Creek from the dinghy. No one followed him. After he disappeared we drove back out to my boat. Holly began preparing her dive gear. We wanted to spend as little time as possible on the site. We wanted to get in, bring up the stash, and get out as fast as possible. John Kipp had been keeping an eye on the area, and the buoys, on his daily fishing trips. He reported no unusual activity.

I punched in the coordinates on the GPS and slowly pulled away from our anchorage. We motored south, past Islamorada, and joined up with the Yacht Channel at Old Dan Bank. I turned to the Northwest. We made our way past Sprigger Bank, and on to Schooner Bank. The next landmark was the Oxford Bank. We rounded the north end of the shallows until we saw marker twelve. Tommy's line ran east to west just below Sandy Key.

I slowed down to a crawl and looked through my binoculars. It took a few minutes, but eventually I spotted a red buoy. I couldn't see the green one, but it didn't matter. We'd found our dive site. I anchored fifty feet from the red buoy. It was barely visible. The red was badly faded and the attached grass weighted it down. It would appear to any fisherman to be an abandoned lobster trap.

I lowered the dinghy and threw in several of my longer dock lines. Holly was suited up and ready to jump in. No other boats were in the vicinity.

"Take the loop end of the line," I told Holly. "Just snap the carabiner through the loop and give me a good tug."

"I'll have to come back up for each box," she said.

"Fine," I said. "You can help me pull it up on your way."

"Rib still bothering you?" she asked.

"It's okay right now," I said. "But I suspect it won't like too much hard labor."

"I'm ready when you are," she said.

"Let's go."

Holly went down with the loop end of the line. I floated in the dinghy above her. She used the trot line to pull herself along. In less than three minutes she was at the first box. I felt the tug and started hauling the line back up. Holly came up with it, pushing from the bottom. Together, we hefted it over the side and into the dinghy.

"One down," she said.

"Five to go," I replied.

Back down she went. The procedure was repeated two more times. Three boxes were enough weight for one trip. We took our loot back to the big boat and returned for the last three boxes. It went like clockwork. There was very little current. No sharks appeared to spoil the works. No pirates showed up, demanding a share of the booty. No curious fishermen slowed down to see what we were up to. We had all six boxes loaded up in less than an hour. Three hundred pounds of gold coins were stored in the hold of *Freedom*. The dive gear was rinsed off and hung to dry. We pulled anchor and left the scene, happy with our efforts. It was the first time that any part of this mission had gone smoothly. I took it as a good sign.

After Holly changed into dry clothes, she joined me on the bridge.

"That was too easy," she said.

"I'm guessing the hard part is going to be selling it," I said.

"You have any ideas?"

"I think Tommy will steer me in the right direction," I said. "But getting the deal done worries me."

"I'm not up for any dangerous shit," she told me. "I told you. I've had enough of that."

"I hear you," I said. "I'll leave you out of it."

"You thinking of doing it yourself?" she asked.

"I've got an idea," I said. "I'll tell you later after I talk to Tommy."

"I hope it's not another one of your hare-brained schemes," she said. "You can't go in winging it and hope shit works out."

"I might be able to enlist some help," I told her.

"This ought to be good," she said.

"I think I'll dust off Winston Shade for the first meeting," I said. "Add a little class to this operation."

"I thought I'd never see him again," she said.

"I've still got the suits and ties," I said. "I think I've got some business cards left too."

I had recently taken on the Winston Shade persona to navigate my way through the seedy world of south Florida politics. It was part of my personal mission to destroy Taylor. I'd really gotten in over my head, but the false identity shielded me from future repercussions. I couldn't use him again in Southwest Florida, but he'd do the job for me in the Keys, or Miami. I wasn't sure where this gold transaction would take place, but Miami seemed like a good bet.

It was late in the day when we anchored back outside Tommy's creek. We left the gold stowed when we went in to pay him a visit. He was waiting for us on the boat.

"Did you have a good day fishing?" he asked.

"Got our limit," I said. "No sweat. Did you have any trouble?"

"I got us some lobsters," he said. "But not until after the Coast Guard left."

"They sent the Coast Guard after you?"

"Indeed," he said. "Four armed young men, very earnest. They pulled their safety inspection on me. Searched the whole boat. Asked a lot of questions about the equipment. Measured the one lobster that I had at the time."

"I take it they left disappointed," I said.

"They found nothing to verify their suspicions," he said. "Just an old fool out chasing lobsters."

"I think we can call today a success," I said. "I've got an extra three hundred pounds of weight in the hold."

"That's just the first step," he said. "I've been making some calls. You'll need to meet an agent of the money man and try to make a deal."

"What trouble should I be looking for?"

"The first meeting will be upfront," he said. "They'll want to see a sample. Verify we've got something they want."

"Then what?"

"The exchange is the problem," he said. "If they think they can get away with it, they'll take the gold and leave you with nothing. Might even take you out so as to not leave any witness."

"I figured that," I said. "I may have a plan."

"Was a time I'd have gone in with you," he said. "But those days are behind me."

"Holly wants no part of it either," I told him.

"How you going to handle it then?" he asked.

"I'm going to try to recruit some help," I said. "I think I know just where to look."

"Let's set up the first meeting," he said. "If it goes well, then you can worry about the rest."

"Fill me in on the details of this gold," I said. "How much money are we talking about?"

Tommy was quick with his figures. This was clearly something he had experience with. At the current exchange rate, we had 6.2 million dollars laying in the bilge of my boat.

"That's a lot of money for a half day's work," I said.

"It was a hell of a lot more than a half day's work," he responded. "It was years of my life.

It was my marriage. I did jail time for that gold. I lost everything."

"You're about to get a piece of it back," I said. "What can we expect them to pay?"

"Probably half at best," he said. "This guy is just a pass-through. Think of him as a broker. He's got to make money off the deal too."

"Sounds a lot like the drug trade," I said. "Everybody gets a piece."

"Exactly," he said. "Other than the moral implications."

"So we're looking at three million or so?"

"I'd like to get four," he said. "He can make a million. His buyer can make a million. You might have to explain that to him. He's going to open up real low, try to steal it from you. You've got to make him think you've got other options, even though you don't."

"How will the final exchange go down?" I asked.

"Like they all do," he said. "Some deserted place that you won't be able to case beforehand. He'll have three or four heavily armed men. They'll be intimidating. You'll be at their mercy, hoping he keeps his end of whatever bargain you made with him."

"I don't like the sounds of that," I admitted.

"That's why you need help," he said. "You walk into an ambush alone, and it's likely over for you. I might give you a minute of grief, but I'd really miss the money that gold would bring. Come up with something good, or I can't let you attempt it. We'll have to figure something else out."

Holly was at the end of her rope with this mission, and me. I wanted it to be over too. I worried about Shirley and how much longer she'd hang on. I couldn't let too much time pass while we figured out some other alternative way to sell the gold. I needed a small army to watch my back. There was only one place in the Keys that I could find such a thing. I needed to go talk to Bald Mark.

Bald Mark was the king of all drug lords in south Florida. Dealers the cops thought were drug lords got their product from him. It hadn't always been that way. He started by using his connections as an ex-cop to control the weed market from Key Largo to Key West. I needed to make a quick score and signed on to run some weed into the Keys with my boat. It all escalated from there. I got into a bind in Cuba, and Mark bailed me out, on the condition that I smuggle a pretty young Cuban girl back to the States. I was in his debt. When he went to prison, I agreed to run all of his drugs. It was a scary time for me and *Leap of Faith*. In order to escape his clutches, and repay my debt, I'd run a ton of cocaine back from Columbia. His business stayed afloat while he did his time. It exploded when he was released. We parted on good terms. Most men who parted ways with Bald Mark ended up in the Everglades with a bullet in their head, or at the bottom of Hawk Channel with cement shoes.

He kept a staff of hard men to carry out his work and enforce his brand of justice to those that wronged him. He was a dangerous man. The goons that he employed were just the type of men I needed. I thought he might agree to help. I knew that it would cost me. Tommy agreed to reimburse me, no matter the fee, once he got his money from the gold. The danger for me would be if we failed. I'd owe Bald Mark. I didn't want to owe Bald Mark. What had begun as a lark to look for Shirley's gold, had evolved into a life-threatening situation. I had a knack for that. It was what Holly disliked about our relationship. I couldn't blame her, but there was no turning back now.

I was shining my dress shoes when Holly returned from the cleaners with my newly pressed business suit. I asked her to sit and talk.

"I don't want you to go," I said. "But I'll completely understand if you do."

"I can't quit now," she said. "I was hoping to make some money in this deal."

"I'm sorry it's turned into this," I said. "You warned me. You were right."

"How does our gold play into Tommy's deal?" she asked.

"Good question," I said. "I'll talk to Tommy about it."

"I'm going to hang around and see this through," she said. "But I'll not catch bullets or otherwise get killed over it."

"Understood," I said. "You've done enough already. Just hang with me a little longer. I'll get you a payday."

"Plus I want to make sure you survive," she said. "Or be there to patch you up when you get hurt. We can't have you getting killed either. I'd miss you."

"If I don't make it," I said. "Take care of my boat. Change the name back before you sell her. I can't have her running around with the wrong name on her."

"Don't talk like that," she said. "You're Breeze. You'll come out of this looking like a genius."

"I appreciate your confidence," I said.

I dressed up as Winston Shade in preparation for the first meeting with the broker. John Kipp picked me up and drove me to a car rental place in Key Largo. I rented a shiny new Black Lincoln Navigator with John's ID. I drove it up US 1 and onto the turnpike towards Miami. I hoped to drive it back without any bullet holes.

I met the man at a rented office in a strip mall in south Miami. It was one of those places you could rent by the day, week, or month. You got a receptionist in the deal. She was dismissed as soon as I entered. We entered a sparsely furnished room and closed the door.

"Mr. Shade," he said, extending his hand. "Thank you for coming."

He was alone. I didn't detect a weapon. This was a simple introduction. There would be no cash or merchandise exchanged. I shook his hand and put a briefcase on the table. I opened it. I had divided the inside into two compartments. On the left, I'd placed a hundred of Tommy's gold coins. On the right were ten of Shirley's gold bars, and two figurines.

"What is this?" he asked, pointing to the right side of the briefcase.

"We are both agents acting on behalf of other parties," I said. "I'm to negotiate the sale of the coins, but I'm making it contingent on the sale of these bars."

"What are they," he asked. "And what of the little gold men?"

"The gold is Pre-Columbian, no doubt," I began. "The figures cannot be properly identified. Believe me, I've tried."

"Are you suggesting they are ancient artifacts?" he asked. "That's not my area of expertise."

"I can't truthfully claim any such thing," I said. "But they are of the same gold. It's roughly ninety percent pure."

"I am not interested in impure gold," he said. "I want the coins. How many more of them do you have?"

"I have three hundred pounds total," I said. "Which I'd be happy to sell to you, after you buy my bars. They are mine and mine alone. They do not belong to the owner of the coins."

"I'm pretty sure I know who that is," he said, pulling out his phone.

"Doesn't matter who it is," I said. "The coins are the coins. Six million dollars' worth."

He appeared to be using the calculator function. He furrowed his brow as he punched the numbers in.

"How many of these bars?" he asked.

"Forty," I told him.

"I don't want the idols," he said. "These types of things are bad for one's life expectancy. They're bad mojo."

"I've heard that," I said. "You'll still have to buy the bars before you can have the coins."

He punched some more numbers into his phone.

"It's insignificant," he said. "The bars are a waste of my time."

"One of the others will take them," I said. "Maybe one of them isn't afraid of little gold men."

"You have other prospects for the coins?" he asked.

"These things are the hottest thing on the market right now," I said. "As soon as the word got out, I had people beating down my door."

"There aren't many people who can make this kind of deal," he said.

"I've got a list of those who I think can," I told him. "Shall I deal with someone else?"

"The man I represent would not be happy," he said. "I'm here to make a deal today."

"Start talking," I said. "I can deliver the rest at your convenience."

He paused for a minute, thinking. He stepped outside to make a phone call. When he came back in I sensed he was ready to deal.

"Two hundred thousand for the bars," he said. "Not a penny more. No deal on the idols. Take them with you."

"I'd like to collect on that before I bring the coins," I told him. "Like I said, it's a separate deal. You've bought the right to negotiate on the coins."

"I can get you the cash before you leave," he said.

"Excellent," I said. "Now, let's get down to business."

He started ridiculously low, just like Tommy had warned me. Eventually, we settled on 3.5 million. He wanted to call me with the details on making the exchange. The business cards I carried had Jimi's number on them. I couldn't remember Holly's number. I took his card and said that I'd call him the next day. I waited while he went out to get my cash. To show good faith, I gave him the coins and bars right there on the spot. I put the cash in the briefcase, along with the unwanted idols.

I felt pretty good on the drive south. Two hundred thousand didn't seem like much for Shirley's gold, but at least I'd gotten rid of it. Something was better than nothing. I could give Shirley one hundred thousand. Holly and I would get fifty each.

I didn't stop in Key Largo. Instead, I continued to Tavernier. I pulled that big Lincoln into the marina where Bald Mark could be found. I got out, straightened my tie, and walked right into the tiki hut where he held court every afternoon. He didn't recognize me at first. His men came to attention while he assessed the situation. I saw the light go on in his eyes. He waved for his men to stand down. The first time I'd met him, I was terrified. He had an intimidating stature. He had muscles upon muscles, with a clean shaven head. He had penetrating black eyes. He was a thug. I'd come to know him over time. He possessed a unique intelligence common among successful gangsters. He ruled with an iron fist, but he would listen to reason. He appreciated intelligence in others, something he didn't get from his hired hands.

"I can't think of a single reason that you'd come back here," he said. "It must be a good one."

"I need muscle and guns," I said. "I figured you'd have plenty of both."

He threw back his head and laughed deep and long. He laughed so hard his eyes watered. Some of his goons chuckled nervously.

"Can you believe this guy?" he said. "I've dealt with some hard cases in my time. This guy's got bigger balls than any of them."

He turned to look at me. The laugh was gone. He bore a hole in me with his black eyes.

"I'll listen to your request," he said. "But like I said, it better be good."

"I need to make an exchange," I said. "My goods for someone else's money. It's not drugs."

"If it was drugs you wouldn't be here," he said. "So what is it?"

"Gold."

"You a treasure hunter now?" he said. "How much money we talking about?"

"Three and a half million," I said.

"Well kiss my ass," he said. "You always were an enterprising son of a bitch. It will be expensive to protect that kind of money."

I asked if we could speak in private. He motioned to his men. They all stepped outside. I wanted to know if I was to pay them directly, or if I was supposed to pay him. He said his guys worked for him. I asked how much. He said a hundred grand. He'd give me five guys for a hundred grand. He'd pay them ten each, make a quick fifty.

"That's a lot of damn money, Mark," I said.

"Where else you going to find what you need?" he asked.

"Look, the gold isn't mine," I said. "I'm arranging the deal. I can get the hundred grand back after we sell the gold."

"I need it upfront," he said. "I can't send these guys into a dangerous situation without getting paid first. I'd also like for all of them to come back in one piece."

Beggars can't be choosers. He had me over a barrel. I had to agree. If the deal went south, I'd be out a hundred grand. If Tommy didn't get his money, he couldn't reimburse me. If Mark's men got shot up, I'd be in deep shit with him. I was only getting out of this thing with the fifty grand I'd get for Shirley's gold. It was hardly worth it, but what else could I do? I'd made a deal with Tommy, just like I'd done with Shirley. I had to stay true to my word.

I agreed to Bald Mark's terms. We shook hands. It hurt just a bit, in more ways than one.

Nineteen

"The team has been assembled," I told Holly and Tommy. "Big, ugly guys with bad attitudes and bad breath."

"What about the meeting with the buyer?" Tommy asked.

"What did you do with Shirley's gold?" Holly asked.

"I got two hundred grand for Shirley's gold," I said. "Three point five for Tommy's. I call to make arrangements for the swap tomorrow. I've got five tough characters to go with me. Not a bad day's work, if I do say so myself."

They both ruminated over the information they'd just received. I knew Tommy had hoped for four million. I knew that the amount I'd gotten for Shirl's gold seemed paltry, but I was satisfied that I'd done the best I could, under the circumstances. This ordeal was drawing to a close. We'd all feel better when it was finished.

"You did okay," said Tommy. "Especially getting some backup. I didn't know you had that kind of connections."

"I didn't either," Holly said. "There seems to be a lot we don't know about Breeze."

"All part of my charm," I joked. "Adds a little mystery."

Holly gave me a look of disapproval. I'm sure she was wondering how I came up with five hard men in just a few hours. I'd been purposely vague about that time in my life with her. At one time, I was a coworker with Mark's former employees. I'd smashed one of their skulls in with a hammer to protect the virtue of that pretty young Cuban girl. I wasn't proud of those days, but the connection was now coming in handy. Tommy was seeing me in a different light as well. I thought that he appreciated my ability to round up resources quickly. He was happy with his decision to join forces with Holly and me. We'd done all the work. He supplied his boat for our gold. We recovered his. Holly had done all the diving. I arranged for the sale. I arranged for the guns and muscle. I was going to make the swap, maybe risking my life in the process. At the end of it all, Tommy would walk away a rich person. Holly and I would not.

What a long, strange trip it had been.

Holly pulled me aside to speak in private. I knew that she wasn't thrilled with how things had worked out. She'd been teased by dreams of untold riches. I'd turned her life upside down for a measly fifty grand. Still, that money would keep her afloat for a long time. It was better than nothing.

"Whatever happens," she said. "You come back here alive. You understand? I'll never be able to live with myself if you don't make it, especially when I'm not going with you."

"I'll be fine," I said. "These guys I got are pretty badass."

"Maybe I should go along," she said. "At least I'd be another gun."

"Absolutely not," I said. "No way in hell. You wait here and keep Tommy company. He seems a bit nervous."

"Shit," she said. "He can't be more nervous than me. Aren't you afraid? Not even a little bit?"

"I can't say I'm not nervous," I admitted. "But I've done everything I can do to keep the odds on our side. I don't think the guy I met is malicious. We'll see what he brings with him. I think it will be okay."

"I hope you're right," she said.

The following morning we transferred Tommy's gold to shore. I made the call. He wanted to meet that night. The meeting place was an abandoned fish house just south of a place called Lakes by the Bay. It wasn't far from Homestead. It was near the turnpike but in a non-residential area. He didn't want to give me time to look the spot over before the deal went down. It was a good strategy on his part.

I called Bald Mark. He promised to send his men to Tommy's mother's place in plenty of time. He wished me luck. We had all afternoon to kill. Tommy paced the deck of his shrimper. Holly chewed her fingernails.

I reclined in a hammock and thought through the situation. I told myself to remain calm. I'd met with the man as Winston Shade. I'd worn an expensive Italian suit, with fancy shoes. We'd negotiated like reasonable businessmen. Sure, he'd bring guns, but I doubted he would anticipate the amount of force I was bringing with me. I hadn't even known that fact when we talked. He had no reason to suspect foul play on my part, but it was prudent of me to make sure that he would live up to his end of the bargain. Unknown variables remained. I couldn't control those. I left Holly to her chewing and Tommy to his pacing and took a nap.

Two black SUV's pulled into the drive at five o'clock. Bald Mark was the first to exit. I was surprised to see him.

"What are you doing here?" I asked.

"I've been thinking about this all day," he said. "I'm coming along, no extra charge."

"You don't have to do that," I said. "It's my gig."

"We do this kind of deal all the time," he said. "We know what we're doing. My guys follow me. I'm going with them this time. You'll get your money and we'll all get out safely."

"How do you want to handle the exchange?" I asked.

"We present immediately with overpowering force," he explained. "We'll control the situation, but you'll make the deal as agreed upon. You won't screw him. You won't get screwed."

"Understood."

Mark's guys helped me load the six boxes of gold coins into the Navigator. Mark rode with me. He didn't have much to say on the trip north. His men followed us. It was just after dark when we drove through the gate of the old fish house. A large black sedan was parked, facing us, with its lights on. I stopped about thirty feet in front of it. His lights went out. I doused mine.

"Here we go," said Mark.

Three men emerged from the sedan. My guy was in the middle. Mark and his men burst out of the cars with automatic weapons drawn. They were on our adversaries in seconds. Mark held a gun to the forehead of the agent, pushing him backward until he hit the hood of his car. The other two men we disarmed and frisked.

"Just do as you're told and nobody gets hurt," said Mark. "We're here to peaceably enforce an agreement."

The agent nodded. The other two shrugged.

"Where's the money?" I asked.

"Where's the gold?" the agent responded.

I had to give it to him. He had cold blue steel pressed against his forehead, but he kept his cool. Mark kept his gun pressed tightly while I went to get the gold. One of Mark's guys assisted me. We had them outnumbered. I presented the boxes, opened each one, and waved my hand over the shiny gold coins.

"The money," I said.

Mark pressed a little harder.

"In the trunk," he said. "Keys in my pocket."

I walked up and took the keys from him. I tossed them to the guy who'd help me carry the gold. He opened the trunk and took out two duffel bags. He dropped them on the ground next to the gold.

"Open them up," I said.

He opened both bags, revealing stacks of cash. I rummaged through the stacks, thumbed a few of them. It looked legit. I motioned to Mark. He ordered his guy to stay with the agent. He inspected the cash too. He nodded to me. Both ends of the bargain had been upheld.

"I appreciate doing business with you," I said.

"This really wasn't necessary," he answered.

"One can never be too careful," I said.

I loaded the cash in the Navigator. Bald Mark and his men released the prisoners. They got their weapons back. We waited as they got in the car and drove off with the gold. It was over.

"We go out with windows down and weapons at the ready," said Mark. "I don't think it's likely, but be ready for an ambush."

We sent one of the other cars out first. I followed. The third car stayed close behind. There was no ambush waiting for us. Once we hit the turnpike and headed south, I relaxed.

"Your crew is pretty quick for big men," I told Mark. "That went as smoothly as could be expected."

"They've had plenty of practice," he said. "In tougher situations than that."

"I didn't know what to expect," I said.

"You did the right thing," he said. "You made sure you were ready, no matter what was thrown at you. Smart thing to do."

"I owe you my thanks," I said. "Even though it came at a steep price."

"I'm a businessman first," he said. "I don't have friends. You included. It was no favor. It was a transaction."

"Always the tough guy," I said.

"Keeps me alive."

All three cars stopped back at Tommy's mother's place. We carried the duffel bags down to the shrimper. Bald Mark and I shook hands. It didn't hurt this time.

"Call me first next time," he said. "I don't like surprise visitors."

"I don't own a phone," I said.

"Get one before you need me again," he advised. "Join the twenty-first century, for crying out loud."

"People keep telling me that," I said.

He got back into one of the SUVs and drove away.

I hoped I'd never need his help again.

Holly and Tommy waited anxiously. They hadn't opened the duffel bags.

"It's all there," I said. "Three and a half million bucks."

"Holly shit, Breeze," said Holly. "You did it."

"Son of a bitch," said Tommy. "I never believed this day would come."

"You're welcome," I said. "You old gold digging bastard."

Tommy stepped inside and returned with a bottle of champagne. We all broke out in giant smiles. Holly gave me a big hug, which I enjoyed. Tommy gave me a big hug, which I didn't. We each took a long pull of the champagne. Holly dumped what was left in the bottle over my head.

"I still don't know how you do it," she said. "But I'll give you props. You got the job done."

"I had a feeling about you," said Tommy. "I sensed that you were a capable individual."

"I'm just glad it's over," I told them. "I need a vacation now. First, I take Shirley her money."

"Speaking of money," said Tommy. "I want you two to take a half million, with one condition."

"That's mighty generous," said Holly.

"What's the condition?" I asked.

"Some of it goes into the kitty to help Shirley," he said. "You can decide how much. You've earned a piece of it."

Holly and I looked at each other. I could see the wheels spinning in her head. She was calculating and reading dollar signs. Maybe this adventure was worth her time after all.

"We can figure it all out later," I said. "Thanks, Tommy. You're okay in my book."

"Give my best to the old gal when you see her," he said.

"What are you going to do with yourself now," I asked him.

"Hunt for gold," he said. "It's all I know how to do."

"Figures," I said. "Stay legal this time. Don't rip anybody off."

"It'll just be a hobby," he said. "I can live on three million till I die."

"If you need a good diver, give me a call," said Holly. "I'm staying down here in the Keys."

I wasn't staying in the Keys. I needed to go find Shirley. I needed to disappear. I'd forgotten all about the FBI. I wasn't sure where I would go, but Holly wasn't going with me. That was apparent. We hauled our money out to my boat. I wanted to sit down and divvy it up properly, but Holly stopped me. She took my hand and led me to my bunk. She put her hands on my chest and pushed me onto the bed. She climbed on top and wriggled out of her clothes. I did the same. She made love to me like she meant it. Afterward, she lay with her head on my chest and we held each other for a long time.

"You're an amazing man, Meade Breeze," she said. "I really want to love you."

"I love you, as best I can," I said. "I wish it was something more."

"I know," she said. "What the hell is wrong with us?"

"Let's just enjoy what we have," I said. "For as long as we have it."

We stayed there holding each other until we fell asleep, and long after.

Twenty

We were all business the next morning. We laid out the seven hundred thousand dollars. It was an impressive pile. I separated the two hundred thousand that came from Shirley's gold. Half of it was hers. I put it in a separate pile. I gave Holly fifty and myself fifty. I moved on to the remaining half million.

"If it's okay with you," I said to Holly. "I'd like to take my expenses off the top."

"No problem," she said. "Have at it."

Tommy had already given me the hundred grand to reimburse what I paid Bald Mark. I'd tucked it away someplace safe. I counted out five grand for Holly's transmission and gave it to her. I laid aside another ten grand for what I'd spent over the course of the mission. I hadn't kept any records. I just estimated. Holly was okay with it. We were left with four hundred and eighty-five thousand dollars, an odd amount to split three ways.

"I say we give Shirley half," I said. "Or close to it."

"How do you figure that," Holly asked. "This is our money. Tommy said we can decide how much to give her."

"We wouldn't have this money if it weren't for Shirley," I said. "This whole caper was her doing from the start."

"Good point," she said. "I'm amenable. Let's say we give her an even two hundred thousand. We split the rest."

"That would total three hundred for her," I said. "I guess that's okay."

"It's settled then," she said. "Divvy it up."

I counted out the stacks and made three piles. We still had an uneven amount. I ended up putting an extra twenty-five thousand in Holly's pile without her knowing. It was just easier that way. I still came out with one hundred and seventy-five grand. Holly had two hundred grand. She'd figure it out later after I was gone.

After we stowed away the cash, we stood and looked at each other. I still had to take her back to Marathon, but our time together was coming to an end. She came to me and we hugged softly.

"Thank you for everything," she said. "Seriously, the money, the adventure, all of it. I know I gave you a hard time about it, but I'm grateful for our time together."

"It doesn't have to end," I said.

"Yes, it does," she said. "At least for now. I need to get away. Spend some time alone."

"I guess I'll be doing the same," I said. "Come on, let's get underway."

It was a quiet trip. We pulled into Boot Key Harbor with heavy hearts. Instead of drawing out our goodbye, I eased up alongside *Another Adventure* close enough for Holly to jump across. I idled nearby, looking back. She stood there waving. I gave her a wave back before throttling up and motoring away. A deep sense of loss came over me. She'd been the central figure in my life for a long time. We just couldn't seem to hold together for some reason. Now she was gone. I hoped it wouldn't be forever.

The mission had been a success otherwise. I was flush with cash. Shirley would be richer too. My little problem with the FBI was the only hitch I could think of. I was alone again, and I needed to keep a low profile, but that was familiar territory for me. I could handle it. I motored slowly back out the channel and under the Seven-mile Bridge. I anchored just off of Keys Fisheries for the night, on the north side of Vaca Key. I had a great view of the sunset, but no one to share it with. I decided to break out Captain Morgan. He never let me down.

I had that dream again. Holly's sails disappeared over the horizon. It didn't keep repeating this time. She just sailed away and that was that. She was gone.

I made good time the next day. I cruised right on past Little Shark River and nearly made it to Goodland before dark. The tide wasn't right, so I anchored near Coon Key Light for the night. I rode the incoming tide the next day up the river to the quaint little settlement of Goodland. Shirley's boat was anchored near the marina, as it had been before. Her dinghy was tied off to the stern. I dropped my hook, put the dinghy in the water, and went over to tell her the good news.

She didn't respond to my calls. I thought she might be napping. I banged on the hull. She didn't answer. Normally, if the dinghy was home, so was the sailor. I tied off and climbed aboard. The companionway door wasn't locked, so I opened it. The smell of death punched me in the chest. I put my shirt over my mouth and nose and peered inside. There was no body. It didn't take a rocket scientist to figure out that Shirley had died here. Someone had found her and the body had been removed. The sense of loss renewed itself. I tried hard not to give in to grief and sentimentality. I was a tough guy, I told myself. I didn't want the feelings, but the double whammy of Holly and Shirley was more than I could handle.

I fought it all off and proceeded to open all the hatches to air the boat out. I wanted to find out what happened to her, but I needed to pull myself together first. I went back to my boat to try to make sense of it all. First Holly, now Shirley. The last few months had been for her. She sent us off on a grand adventure, all due to her fixation with finding treasure. She didn't live long enough to fully realize her dream. I had looked forward to handing her a big stack of cash. It had motivated me to keep moving after parting ways with Holly. I had a picture in my mind of her face when I showed her all that money.

I sat on my back deck feeling sorry for myself. I wouldn't let the tears come, even though no one would see me cry. What was I supposed to do now? I don't know why it took me so long, but I finally figured it out. I had to find Shirley's daughter. I needed to track her down and give her the money. That's what Shirley wanted it for in the first place. That's what I had signed up for. The mission wasn't over yet.

I drove into the marina with a sense of purpose. I was certain that a dead body would be the talk of the town. I asked the first person I saw on the docks.

"What happened to Shirley?"

"Probably a heart attack," he said. "Maybe just old age."

"Where did they take her?" I asked.

"I don't know," he said. "The coroner was here. An ambulance took the body soon after."

"Was she properly identified?" I asked. "Next of kin notified?"

"You'd have to ask the sheriff," he said. "None of us here knew her last name, but they went out to the boat and found her ID."

I realized that I didn't know her last name either. I also knew that I couldn't walk into a sheriff's office asking questions. I wasn't next of kin. They might want to know who I was. There had to be clues on her boat. I needed to go back out there. I could look for an address book or something. I hoped that the smell had subsided.

It wasn't quite as bad, but it was still disturbing. The meaning behind the odor was what was getting to me. I dug around in Shirl's little sailboat, looking for clues. I came across her cash box. Almost all of the money I had given her earlier was still there. She had hardly spent any of it. I did find a half bottle of rum and a carton of cigarettes. That was her idea of splurging. There was no address book. There were no letters or any kind of mail. She had a few cans of beans and a bag of rice in the pantry. It was sad, really. She had twenty thousand dollars, but no food. I sat down at her little table and looked around. I spotted a cell phone. It was plugged into a twelve-volt outlet, fully charged. I opened her contacts. There were only three. She had saved the numbers of Molly, Doctor, and Dave. Molly had to be her daughter.

I pressed send and listened to the ring.

"Hello".

"Is this Molly, Shirley's daughter?" I asked.

"Who is this?" she asked. "She just passed away you know."

"My name is Breeze," I told her. "I was your mother's friend."

"Well she died on that stupid old boat," she said. "You can have it. I don't want the damned thing. I told her this would happen someday. She wouldn't listen."

"Just give me a minute," I said. "Your mother loved you very much. She left you something. She left you money, lots of it."

"I don't know how she could have done that," she said. "She only had her social security. She lived like a hobo."

"She found her gold, Molly," I said. "She looked for treasure her entire life, and she finally found it. She wanted you to have the money."

"How much?"

"Three hundred thousand and change," I said.

There was a long pause.

"Molly? You there?"

"I don't know what to say," she said. "That's a lot of money. I think I'm in shock."

"She made me promise to get it to you," I said. "I helped her sell the gold. She was adamant that you get the money. I guess you could call it her last wish."

"That crazy old woman," she said. "She really found gold?"

"Maybe not so crazy after all," I suggested. "She was my friend. I'll miss her."

"I've been missing her for years," she said. "She didn't come around much."

"She lived life on her terms," I said. "I'm kind of the same way. We understood each other."

"Can you come to Englewood?" she asked. "I'd like to meet with you. And there's the money."

"I'll bring the money," I said. "I have to honor her wishes."

"Anybody in their right mind would just keep it for themselves," she said. "Nobody knew she had any money."

"I've often been accused of not being in my right mind," I said. "But I made a promise."

"No wonder you two were friends," she said. "You must live on a boat too."

"That's correct," I said. "It will take me a couple days to get to Englewood. I can anchor in Chadwick Cove."

"I'll meet you at Flounder's," she said. "Call me when you get there."

"Will do."

"Thank you very much for getting in touch," she said. "Thanks for being my mother's friend."

I'd found her. It was an easy run up to Englewood. The money changed her tune. I didn't know what would become of Shirl's old boat, but I had more important matters to attend to. It wasn't worth much anyway. It had been Shirley's whole world, but it had no value to anyone else. I took the phone and charger with me. I could still make it as far as Fort Myers Beach before dark.

I took the back way to Marco Island and used Capri Pass to enter the Gulf. I ran just offshore for five hours until I neared Matanzas Pass. The water turned dark and murky. They must have still been releasing water from Lake Okeechobee into the Caloosahatchee River. I'd done my best to bring attention to the problem but little had been done to correct it. I was just one man. It would take political will to make a difference. I didn't have time for it this time around. I needed to stay well out of the eye of the public. I'd run up to Chadwick Cove, make the cash delivery, and disappear.

I had rounded Bowditch Point and was heading for the bridge when I saw it. There was a familiar looking Hatteras tied up at Pink Shell Marina. It was Incognito. Captain Fred was back in Florida. He'd been thoroughly involved in my little misadventure in the

Bahamas. He'd saved Taylor's life. He stayed behind while I ran. He'd visited her in the hospital. He was the one who warned me about the FBI. I had to talk to him.

I couldn't play around in Fort Myers Beach for long. I needed to get on up to Englewood, so as soon as I grabbed a mooring ball, I put the dinghy in and headed for Fred's boat.

"Ahoy, Captain Fred," I yelled as I pulled alongside.

"Jesus, Mary, and Joseph," he responded. "I'll be God-damned."

"Fancy meeting you here," I said. "Permission to come aboard?"

"You have a habit of popping up at the strangest times and places," he said. "I didn't see you come in."

"My boat is in disguise," I said. "Incognito, if you will."

"If you had a phone," he said. "You'd already know that's not necessary."

"I need to join the twenty-first century, I know," I said. "What the hell are you talking about?"

"Come inside," he said. "I've got a story for you."

Captain Fred was a great story teller, but he was known to embellish. I knew better than to press him to get to the point. He offered me a beer and a seat in the main salon.

"I'm all ears," I said. "I hope it's good news."

"The FBI got Taylor all turned around," he began. "They hit her with a first-degree murder charge. Pressed her to cooperate to avoid the death penalty."

Taylor had pulled a scam on some wealthy investors. She'd used a financial advisor to park their money offshore, gotten the account information, and stolen all of it. She killed the financial guy on her way out the door. She'd run to Captain Fred in the Exumas. I had been the one who'd introduced them. I'd also been the one to track her down. That's when Holly shot her. She had originally told the FBI that it was me who pulled the trigger. It was a mess I'd prefer to forget, but I couldn't with the FBI looking for me.

"They gave her computer access so she could help them recover the money," said Fred. "All of it was returned. In order to mount a legal defense, she tried to access her own account. There was nothing there."

"Her account was empty?"

"He left her ten cents."

"Who?" I asked.

"Your pal Jimi," he said. "There was a message from the bank. It said Mr. Dinapoli appreciates your generous contribution."

"Jimi D. stole all of Taylor's own money?" I asked.

"Almost a million bucks," he said. "The investors all got repaid, but Taylor was left with nothing."

"She lost," I said. "I got her, and Jimi got her. He was last seen in Grand Cayman, probably making a cash withdrawal."

"She couldn't take it," he said. "It was the final straw. You were not supposed to win. You, the hopeless boat bum, had defeated her. Jimi D. wasn't supposed to win either. She was smarter than the both of you, until she wasn't."

"So she gave up?"

"She begged for mercy," he said. "Said she didn't know who shot her, but it wasn't you.

She couldn't recover the stolen money fast enough. She's holding out for a chance of parole. Maybe she'll get thirty or forty years and die a free woman."

"And I'm off the hook?"

"That's right son," he said. "I would have called you."

"If I had a phone, got it," I said. "Maybe I can get one, now that I'm a free man."

"The way you live," he said. "The law will probably be after you again, sooner or later. You should really consider a change of lifestyle."

"I'll take it under advisement," I told him. "I really don't know what's next for me. It's nice to know I'm not wanted, though."

"Why don't you stick around here for a while," he said. "Chase the barmaids and relax a little."

"I'd love to, but I got someplace to be," I said.

"It's like talking to a ghost," he said. "Poof. He's here. Poof. He's gone again."

"I'll look you up when I finish what I've got to do," I said. "It really is good to see you."

"Always nice to be the bearer of good news," he said. "Now what did you do with that rasta blonde you had with you?"

"Long story," I said. "I'll fill you in when I get back."

"Run her off didn't you?"

"Something like that."

Twenty-one

I made my way up to Englewood and anchored in Chadwick Cove. I called Molly. We agreed to meet at Flounder's the next afternoon. I bagged up her cash and killed time watching some goofy old dude dance in his backyard. He played his music loud, too loud. He bopped around the sea wall casting a fishing rod and dancing his ass off. I guessed he didn't like me anchoring behind his house. I found him quite entertaining, even though I didn't like his choice of music. He didn't give up until well after dark.

Molly was my age, and not bad to look at. I could see her mother's features in her face. She had the same color hair, blonde smattered with gray. She lacked the leathery skin and Popeye forearms of Shirley, but she was clearly her mother's daughter. I had no trouble identifying her in the bar. We ordered drinks and sat in the shade. I wanted to hand over the bag and split, but she wanted to talk.

I ended up telling her a few stories. I told her how we'd first met, and how we managed to run into each other in various places over the years. I told her about the gold bars and the curious gold statues that went with them. I asked her if she wanted the little idols too. She said no, that I should keep them. I wondered if she thought they were bad juju like everyone else. We eventually ran out of things to say. The silences grew long. She had her money. I'd done my job. I'd fulfilled my promise to Shirley. I'd been true to my word.

We said our polite goodbyes and I got up to leave.

"Breeze?" she said. "You keep my number you hear? If you ever need someone to talk to."

"Thanks," I said. "You never know."

"My thanks to you," she said. "I really can't thank you enough."

"Do me a favor," I said. "Honor your mother's memory. Buy her a nice headstone or something."

"It's the least I could do."

I left her sitting there with half a drink in her hand. I couldn't decide if a weight had been lifted or more had been added. I was satisfied with what I had done, but I was sadder than ever. It was all over. My work was done. The mission was complete. Holly was gone. Shirley was gone. On the other hand, I was free. When it came down to it, freedom was what it was all about. There was no one left to count on me. I could do whatever I pleased, as soon as I figured out what that was.

I fired up the old boat, pulled the anchor, and cruised out of Chadwick Cove. There was no sign of the dancing fool. I turned south. Pelican Bay was only a few hours away. As I passed by Palm Island Marina, I wondered where Jimi was. I wished him well, that tricky bastard.

I was going home once again. I knew I'd find solace there. I passed under the new bridge at Gasparilla Island. I motored along the inside of the island, past the golf course, and into the Boca Grande Pass. I remembered the idols. They were still packed in rags, down in the bilge. I turned on the autopilot and went down to get them. They looked innocent enough, but everyone kept warning me that they were bad luck. I'd been carrying them around all this time. Maybe they were to blame for the things that had gone wrong. I wasn't really the superstitious type, but why tempt fate?

I punched in the numbers for the spot where we'd found them. I slowed to idle speed when I got there. One by one, I dropped the little gold men overboard. Let someone else find them someday. They can have the bad luck that comes with them. Just as I tossed the last one, I spotted the dorsal fin of a big hammerhead shark. Old Hitler was coming to inspect the new additions to his domain. I should have heeded his warning in the first place. I gave him a salute before throttling up and heading for the entrance to Pelican Bay.

I dropped anchor in my usual spot. I sat on the back deck in my usual spot. I put my feet up on the transom and listened to the silence. Then the usual sounds made themselves known. I heard the chirp on an osprey. I heard the breath of a dolphin. Little wavelets lapped at the hull. Mullet jumped in the shallows.

I just sat still, taking it all in. I began the process of unwinding. I relaxed. Then a realization hit me. There was still something I had to do. I lowered the dinghy and looked at the name on the transom. *Freedom* was a good name, but it had to go. I'd been true to Shirley. I'd been true to Tommy. I'd done my best to be true to Holly. I couldn't forget about *Leap of Faith*.

There was one more thing that had to be done before this trip was finally over. The name on the transom would be erased and replaced.

Long live *Leap of Faith*.

Author's Thoughts

I had a bit of trouble while writing **True Breeze**. It had nothing to do with the plot. Early on, I broke a rib while working on the boat, so I decided to insert it into the storyline. Before I could properly heal, I caught a cold. I was dealing with so much discomfort, I had a hard time keeping my thoughts together when I sat down to write.

The cold hung on for weeks. The pain in my side was slow to diminish. Eventually, I recovered. I'd been thinking through the story, and I had so much in my head that I needed to type. The closing days went quickly.

Old Shirley is a real person. I haven't seen her in over a year, but far as I know, she's still out there, bumming rum and smokes.

Just days before I finished, the real-life Holly showed up and spent the night aboard the real-life *Leap of Faith*. It was great to catch up with her. *Another Adventure* is anchored at Stock Island.

Jimi D. is splitting time between his land-based home and his sailboat, *Whole Nine Yards.*

Captain Fred is still living aboard *Incognito,* at Pink Shell Marina, in Fort Myers Beach.

I just know that there is some gold somewhere around Cayo Costa. Shirley told me so. Maybe someday I'll find it.

Acknowledgements

Cover art: http://dianneparksart.com/

Cover Design: https://ebooklaunch.com/

Interior Formatting: https://ebooklaunch.com/

Editing: John Corbin

Special thanks to beta readers; Dave Calhoun, Jeanene Olson, and Laura Spink

Other Books in the Series

Trawler Trash: http://amzn.to/2fJqvsv

Following Breeze: http://amzn.to/2fXJgq2

Free Breeze: http://amzn.to/2fXILfv

Redeeming Breeze: http://amzn.to/2gbBjAx

Bahama Breeze: http://amzn.to/2fJiMe6

Cool Breeze: http://amzn.to/2ftC0G4

Other Books by Ed Robinson

Leap of Faith; Quit Your Job and Live on a Boat
http://amzn.to/2fFeJwh

Poop, Booze, and Bikinis
http://amzn.to/2gPe54a

The Untold Story of Kim
http://amzn.to/2fFe4uy

Made in the USA
Middletown, DE
26 December 2016